Days at the Torunka Café

Also by Satoshi Yagisawa

Days at the Morisaki Bookshop
More Days at the Morisaki Bookshop

Days at the
Torunka Café
A Novel

Satoshi Yagisawa

Translated from the Japanese by Eric Ozawa

HARPER PERENNIAL

NEW YORK • LONDON • TORONTO • SYDNEY • NEW DELHI • AUCKLAND

HARPER ● PERENNIAL

Without limiting the exclusive rights of any author, contributor or the publisher of this publication, any unauthorized use of this publication to train generative artificial intelligence (AI) technologies is expressly prohibited. HarperCollins also exercise their rights under Article 4(3) of the Digital Single Market Directive 2019/790 and expressly reserve this publication from the text and data mining exception.

This is a work of fiction. Names, characters, places, and incidents are products of the author's imagination or are used fictitiously and are not to be construed as real. Any resemblance to actual events, locales, organizations, or persons, living or dead, is entirely coincidental.

Originally published as 純喫茶トルンカ in Japan in 2022 by Tokuma Shoten Publishing Co., Ltd. Arranged with Tokuma Shoten Publishing Co., Ltd., through Emily Books Agency LTD. and Casanovas & Lynch Literary Agency.

DAYS AT THE TORUNKA CAFÉ. Copyright © 2022 by Satoshi Yagisawa. English translation copyright © 2025 by Eric Ozawa. All rights reserved. Printed in the United States of America. No part of this book may be used or reproduced in any manner whatsoever without written permission except in the case of brief quotations embodied in critical articles and reviews. For information, address HarperCollins Publishers, 195 Broadway, New York, NY 10007. In Europe, HarperCollins Publishers, Macken House, 39/40 Mayor Street Upper, Dublin 1, D01 C9W8, Ireland.

HarperCollins books may be purchased for educational, business, or sales promotional use. For information, please email the Special Markets Department at SPsales@harpercollins.com.

hc.com

FIRST US EDITION

Designed by Jackie Alvarado

Library of Congress Cataloging-in-Publication Data
Names: Yagisawa, Satoshi, 1977- author | Ozawa, Eric translator
Title: Days at the Torunka Cafe: a novel / Satoshi Yagisawa; translated from the Japanese by Eric Ozawa.
Other titles: 880-02 Junkissa Torunka. English
Description: First US edition. | New York, NY: HarperPerennial, 2025.
Identifiers: LCCN 2025021101 | ISBN 9780063445857 trade paperback | ISBN 9780063445871 ebook
Subjects: LCGFT: Novels
Classification: LCC PL877.5.A348 J8613 2025 | DDC 895.63/6--dc23/eng/20250520
LC record available at https://lccn.loc.gov/2025021101

25 26 27 28 29 LBC 5 4 3 2 1

Days at the
Torunka Café

Part One

Sunday Ballerinas

It was on a Sunday afternoon, near the end of the year, when a strange woman named Chinatsu Yukimura first appeared at the Torunka Café.

Perhaps because everyone else was busy getting ready for New Year's, the café had been deserted all day long. Around noon, one of the regulars who lived nearby stopped in, but after that there were no more customers, and the only people in the café were me, the owner (his name is Isao Tachibana, but I always call him the owner) and his daughter Shizuku. Outside the windows, the sun was shining brightly, but inside the café, tucked away in an alley a few steps from the busy street of shops and markets, the light was already fading.

We could hear the steady ticking of the pendulum clock on the wall and the sound of a Chopin piano piece playing from the speakers, the volume so low it was barely noticeable.

"Slow day, right?" Shizuku said as she sat lazily behind the counter, reading the sports page a customer had left behind. She'd already said the same thing at least thirty times since we opened that morning.

"Slooow day," I repeated for probably the twenty-eighth or

twenty-ninth time, as I pretended to mop the floor. Shizuku liked to call herself the poster girl of the Torunka Café, and she probably would've said so even if she saw what she looked like flipping through the sports page with her chin resting in her hand and her mouth half open.

"It's because it's the end of the year." Apparently, there weren't any articles capable of holding a high school girl's attention because, after making a lot of noise folding the newspaper in half, Shizuku threw it down on the counter.

"It's got to be because of the end of the year," I said listlessly, still holding the mop and staring off into space with nothing to do. I admit I was a little curious about the pictures of naked women inside the sports section that she'd tossed aside, but it seemed a bit too soon to reach for it, so I held off.

"Hey, Shizuku, sit properly if you're going to sit in that chair. Anybody can see your underwear." The owner, who had been on the other side of the counter, amusing himself polishing the glasses, shot her a disgusted look. To look at him, the owner seemed stern, even a little scary, but he was soft-spoken and rarely revealed his feelings. Even on a day as slow as this, his expression didn't change at all. He devoted his attention to polishing the glasses and cups, an act that made pleasant little squeaking sounds now and then.

"Dirty old man," Shizuku said and stuck her tongue out at him, but the owner seemed unfazed.

"No one wants to look at your underwear," he said rather coldly. "Clean up your act."

A chocolate-brown cat was walking along the concrete wall outside the window, taking delicate little steps as the pale winter sun shone on its back. It was a tomcat I'd seen many times; he slept in the back alley. The front of the café was a thoroughfare for the cats in the neighborhood. The short, fat tail on this one, held straight up, was a testament to all the battles and struggles he'd survived.

I'd read somewhere in a book a long time ago that this downtown area in Tokyo had a lot of stray cats, but it was only after I started working here part time that I made the acquaintance—if that's the right word—of a number of them. Now, I wondered how many of them would make it through the harsh winter this year.

"I wish something interesting would happen."

"Hey," the owner said, looking dumbfounded again. "How do you expect something interesting to happen? If you want something to be interesting, the important thing is to start by living your life fully every day. Then things will start looking interesting all by themselves."

"Don't be so serious. I was just wishing for something to chase away the boredom. Shūichi, you've been wishing for the same thing, right?"

"I have."

"Should've known. My part-timers are hopeless." The owner let out a big sigh, which Shizuku completely ignored. She turned to look at me.

"Shūichi, are you on winter break?"

"For a while now. You're not off yet?"

"Not yet. We still have two more days. What have you been doing over break?"

"Hm? Reading, taking naps, drinking."

"So pretty much the same thing you always do, then."

"You could say that."

"Being a college student sounds like a pretty easy life."

"That's not fair to the other college students in this world. There are a lot of good students out there who have their act together."

"So, you're one of the bad ones, then."

"Oh, I'm one of the bad ones," I said proudly.

"It sounds nice being a bad college student. That's what I want to be. Okay, that settles it. When I graduate high school, I'm going to become a bad college student."

"Well, I wish you luck. I'll strive every day to set an example for you."

"Hey, Shūichi! Don't be a bad influence on Shizuku. You're going to be a senior next year, aren't you? Pretty soon, you're going to have to . . ."

Fortunately, just as the owner was about to start his sermon, the bell on the door jingled, and the door opened. All at once, the three of us turned our heads in that direction, like a goose and her goslings.

A woman appeared in the doorway.

She was fairly young, a rare thing at a café where many of the customers were elderly. She was dressed in a heavy black coat with a bright scarlet scarf; she was small in stature and seemed very quiet. She wore her black hair elegantly cut in a longish bob. It must've been cold outside because her pale cheeks were slightly flushed.

Shizuku sprang up from her chair, quickly ran her fingers through her long hair, and retied her apron. Then she called out "Welcome!" as the sullen look on her face gave way to a professional smile to greet our new customer.

The young woman seemed to hesitate when she realized that with no other customers she had our undivided attention. She looked down and fiddled with her hair.

She was almost like a young deer, so out of fear of startling her, I sidled back into the kitchen like a crab retreating into its burrow.

Shizuku led her to the table farthest in the back and brought her a glass of water. After a conversation so quiet that they seemed to be sharing confidences, Shizuku finally came back with her order.

"One Colombian."

"Coming right up."

The owner milled the beans in the grinder, poured the grinds into the filter, and then began pouring boiling water over them as the room filled with the rich aroma of coffee. Breathing in that aroma while the melody of the piano nocturne drifted through the café, I seemed to lose my grip on reality, and I felt instead like I was walking through the old streets of a European city.

Outside the window another cat was passing by. As I watched it, the owner moved silently through the phases of extracting the flavor from the grounds, and before I knew it, the cup of black, lustrous liquid was ready, the steam rising faintly above it. It's no exaggeration to say that the coffee the owner made was delicious. And yet, despite the fact that Shizuku was born the daughter of a coffee master, she hated coffee and never drank it.

It always seemed like such a waste. If I'd been in her position, I would have been happily drinking coffee from childhood.

"Shūichi."

The owner placed the white porcelain cup filled to the brim

with black liquid and gestured with his chin for me to take it away.

Up to this point, there was nothing too out of the ordinary here, aside from the fact the day had been strangely slow. It was a normal afternoon at the Torunka Café.

But...

The moment I placed the cup of coffee on the table, the young woman, who until then had kept her eyes lowered, looked up at me.

Then, for some reason, her large eyes opened even wider, and she stared intensely at me. Her eyes were radiating such intensity that I had the uneasy feeling that she could see inside me.

She stood abruptly, and I felt a chill as she took my hands in her cold, firm grip. Before I could react to this sudden turn of events, she looked at me and said in a voice overcome with emotion, "We meet at last."

I'm positive that's what she said.

With her holding my hands, I couldn't do anything but stare back at her vacantly in response. For a moment, the café was plunged into silence.

"Um, uh, are you a friend of Shūichi's?" Shizuku, who had retreated into the kitchen, had now returned at full speed, and was looking back and forth between us.

I shook my head violently from side to side. "I don't think so."

I looked at her again and searched my memory. Was she a girl from campus, someone from the neighborhood, a distant relative... I had absolutely no recollection of ever having seen the woman in front of me.

"Um..." I said, trying nonchalantly to shake myself free. But she still held my hands tightly with her cold, pale fingers.

"I'm sorry, could you tell me your name? I apologize if I'm drawing a blank here, but have we met before?"

"No, we haven't," she said, in a tone that was quiet but definitive. It hit me with such force that I felt myself unconsciously take a half step back. "But I've known you for a very long time."

"Huh?"

"My name is Chinatsu Yukimura."

"Oh, um, my name is Shūichi Okuyama."

"Nice to meet you."

"Ni-nice to meet you too . . . ?"

My brain was completely overwhelmed. When something so inconceivable actually happens to you, you're so shocked you don't know how to respond. Shizuku was staring at us with her mouth open, watching to see how things developed.

"This is our first time meeting in this life. We knew each other in a previous life."

"Previous life?"

"We . . ." She stopped talking for a moment, then smiled, her cheeks turning red as if she suddenly felt embarrassed. Then she whispered as if she were sharing a precious secret, "In a previous life, we were lovers." She played with her bangs, looking self-conscious again, and let out a little laugh.

The sun was setting and the café was soon lit up by the amber light of the lanterns. And for some reason, in that dim light, I was sitting down with the woman I knew as Chinatsu Yukimura. It was all because of Shizuku blurting out, "Well, there's no point in standing around talking." Shizuku had grabbed hold of my arm as I was trying to flee and plopped down beside me in a chair.

She was clearly enjoying this.

"I'm, um, really not a shady person..." Chinatsu said, in the shadiest way possible. And yet she seemed for the most part to have regained her composure since she first saw me. She spoke in the near whisper that she'd used when she first came into the café.

"So, Chinatsu, can I call you that? Chinatsu, um, so you really didn't know Shūichi until a moment ago, right?" Shizuku asked, her friendly disposition on display again.

"Yes, I didn't know him."

"But you had met him in a previous life."

"That's right."

Miss Yukimura glanced up at me as if studying my face. "You mean you don't remember?"

"No. And I, um, didn't understand a single word of what you were saying a moment ago," I said, without hiding my discomfort. Shizuku responded by elbowing me as hard as she could under the table.

I glared at her indignantly— *You could've broken my ribs!*—but she merely gestured with her chin toward Chinatsu. Chinatsu hung her head, showing clearly that for her it might as well be the end of the world. I scratched my temple and gave a little sigh.

"So how did we come to know each other?"

"It was in Paris, in a turbulent time: the end of the eighteenth century, right in the middle of the French Revolution."

Her expression transformed in an instant. Her eyes glittered.

"Whoa!" Shizuku made a strange animal-like yowl. It didn't seem to bother Chinatsu though, and she continued her story.

"I've missed you, Sylvie..."

"Eh?"

"Sylvie. That was your name before."

"I was a woman?"

"Yes."

Chinatsu nodded, smiling from ear to ear.

"Whoa," Shizuku yowled again.

"In this previous life, I was a man by the name of Etienne Apert. And you were a girl named Sylvie Soleil, as lovely as a little bird, but with the courage to make even a seasoned soldier pale in comparison."

Though I could imagine Shizuku's reaction, when I snuck a glance at the counter, I saw that even the owner was looking down, and his shoulders were trembling with laughter.

"The first time we met, Sylvie, you were still an innocent eighteen-year-old, but inside you was a spirit that burned with—"

"Okay, I think I get it. Can we please skip ahead?" Just listening to her, I could feel my face turning red.

"I was a poor chimney sweep. The first time I saw you was in the Jardin de Luxembourg. From the moment I laid eyes on you on your way home from school, I was spellbound."

"Whoa!" my high school–age coworker cried out again.

"All I could think about day and night was how to speak to you on your way home from school. I waited in the Jardin du Luxembourg every day for you to walk by on your way home. And then one day, one fateful day, there was a sudden rain shower, and I noticed your slender shoulders were getting wet from the rain, so I rushed to your side holding an umbrella—"

"I see," I said, flustered, brusquely cutting her off in the midst of her increasingly elaborate story.

"That's enough about that part of the story. I can imagine the rest. Basically, the two of us—Sylvie and Etienne, was it? Those two were lovers, then. That's what you're saying, right?"

"Um, yes, that's right. For us to meet again now . . . is truly a miracle."

Before I knew it, her eyes were welling up with tears. She took out a rather girlish pink handkerchief from her bag and gently dabbed the corners of her eyes with it.

"Even if you truly remember this past life, how can you be sure enough to swear that I am that person?"

"That's because . . . the moment our eyes met, I felt it instantly."

"You're saying you think it's fate?" Shizuku said, on the edge of her seat.

"That's . . . right." Chinatsu Yukimura gave an embarrassed smile and took a sip of her coffee. Then she pulled her bangs forward as if to hide her blushing.

"I was just a chimney sweep with no education to speak of, and you were so intelligent, and you had such a fierce sense of purpose. You gently instructed me in the horrors of monarchism, and the potential of the philosophy of the Enlightenment, and you persuaded me that what mattered above all else was that we stood up for ourselves as a people. We yearned for the fall of the *ancien régime*, and we joined the masses revolting against it."

"*Ancien?*"

Shizuku and I gave her a confused look, but then the owner, who had been quiet until that moment, spoke up. "The *ancien régime* was the social order in France at the time, an absolute monarchy with Louis XVI on the throne. You two should try studying history a bit more."

Chinatsu looked at the owner and smiled. "You know it well," she said. "And this coffee is quite delicious."

"Oh no, not really," the owner said, "but thank you very much." He gave an embarrassed smile.

Shizuku looked fed up and mumbled, "Dirty old man." Chinatsu didn't seem to pay her any mind and turned back to me again.

"We might have been insignificant citizens, but our hearts burned brightly with the light of hope and freedom. Yet the path ahead of us was steep. And there were many among us who shed blood in those battles. The decomposing bodies of our comrades were piled in heaps in the city streets . . ." She closed her eyes and gently shook her head like she was grieving their deaths.

"The fighting intensified, and finally I too was detained by government troops. I soon ended up in prison. Even as I approached the end, I never stopped praying that the Revolution would succeed. And, of course, I never forgot you, not even for a moment, Sylvie. The thought of dying and leaving you all alone . . . We swore we'd be together for the dawn of the Revolution; we swore if all fell to ruin, we'd be together then too. And yet . . ."

She covered her face in her hands and burst into tears at last.

"Sylvie," she went on, "I'm sorry. I only wanted to beg your forgiveness."

I thought to myself then that in the twenty-one years I had been on this earth, I had never come across a situation this absurd. Right in front of me was a weeping woman whom I had absolutely no memory of ever having met. I was so utterly baffled by everything that I almost gave in to the impulse to stand up and shout, "Oh I remember!" A woman's tears can be that terrifying.

I held strong and suppressed the urge. If I let that happen, then I'd really be out of my depth. Even when she asked again, "You really don't remember any of it?" I just silently shook my head.

"Hey, Sylvie," Shizuku said, "aren't you being awfully cold!? Isn't there some way for you to remember Etienne?"

Shizuku, who seemed even more moved by Chinatsu's tears, urged me to respond.

Nonetheless, the two of us remained as far apart as ever. Around the time the world outside our windows turned dark blue, two sets of customers came in, one after the other, and she and I got up from our seats.

"I, um, apologize for barging in like this," Chinatsu said in the end as she tried to flee.

"Chinatsu, please come back anytime. You'll see, Shūichi might remember." The poster girl of the Torunka Café couldn't stop herself from taking things a step too far.

"You . . . you wouldn't mind?"

"Of course not!"

Chinatsu, who had up until a moment ago been shedding tears, was now suddenly beaming like a child on her birthday.

"Thank you so much. That makes me happy."

Good grief. I sighed. But I didn't have it in me to overturn the decision of the poster girl of the Torunka Café. Shizuku saw Chinatsu Yukimura off at the door, then she turned to the owner, with a triumphant look on her face, and sneered, "Something interesting did happen after all."

The café was closed for the holidays, so I spent the following days in my cheap, painfully small apartment with no real plans.

My friends from college had all gone home to their families or left on trips. But because of my particular situation, I wasn't heading home to the countryside. I hadn't gone back once since I arrived in Tokyo for college, and my parents hadn't made any great effort to contact me either. I didn't particularly mind. I wasn't looking for that kind of trouble.

On TV, there were only rowdy New Year's shows that I found

painfully boring, but I went on watching anyway. If I showed any initiative at all that day, it was just to get up and make myself a cup of coffee. Starting my part-time job at the café had inspired me to create my own setup at home with an electric grinder and a drip bag to make coffee for myself. At first I didn't really taste the difference, to be honest, but as the owner taught me the basics, I gradually came to see what separated a properly made cup of coffee from everything else.

According to the owner, the type of beans you choose and the quality of your equipment both determine the quality of the coffee, but the secret to making good coffee comes down to "taking the time to do it right."

Simply paying careful attention to the timing of when I removed the filter from the carafe made a marked improvement in the flavor of the coffee. As soon as I became aware of the differences in flavor, I was amazed to compare the owner's coffee with what I made at home. Even with the same type of coffee beans, the aftertaste was totally different.

Once I realized that, the coffee I made improved considerably. It's not like I'm planning on opening my own café in the future, but there's nothing better than a delicious cup of coffee. I don't have any other hobbies or special skills to speak of. There's no harm in being a little bit proud of the coffee I make. It's still far from being up to the level of the owner's, but I think I'm now able to make a decent cup at home.

But this New Year's, no matter what I tried, the coffee I made at home alone seemed tasteless.

Last New Year's, I'd spent the whole day with Megumi. On New Year's Eve we didn't bother going out in the cold, we stayed under the heated kotatsu and greeted the New Year on TV. After midnight, I prepared coffee, and we made a toast to celebrate the new year with the Hagi ware coffee cups we'd splurged on.

I can't say the coffee I made then was delicious, yet as we drank it together, Megumi smiled and said, "It's nice to spend New Year's this way." I can still vividly remember her smile and the sound of her voice then.

Megumi and I broke up about three months ago. Or rather, I got dumped. And for a long time after that, I was a shell of myself. Even the people around me could see I was in a terrible state. As a result, I caused a lot of trouble for the owner and his daughter at the Torunka Café, especially Shizuku, who still worries about me to this day.

Yet I still think about Megumi all the time. Perhaps it wouldn't have mattered who it was, because the first person you go out with will always have a special hold on your heart. Or perhaps I can't forget her simply because I loved her like crazy. Or maybe it's just that I'm the kind of guy who clings to the past. I think three months is a tricky length of time—it's too early to forget someone, but long enough that it's pathetic to go on obsessing over someone you've lost.

Which reminds me: the day Megumi and I started going out was the first day I came to the Torunka Café.

It was two years ago, near the end of the summer after my first year in college.

We decided to stop somewhere on our way home from campus like we always did. We got along well somehow and were often together, at school and off campus, just the two of us, but our relationship wasn't clearly defined. What I mean is we were something more than friends then but not quite girlfriend and boyfriend, and we stayed in that in-between state for a long time.

That day, Megumi wanted to go downtown, so we went to the Yanaka Ginza market street not far from my apartment. It was right at dusk, and the street was busy, full of people looking for something for dinner. There was something peculiar about that street, which had held on to so much of the Shōwa period atmosphere. As we walked down the vibrant, narrow street, the place felt both very nostalgic and very much alive.

We bought fried croquettes from a shop and stuffed our faces as we walked. We were about halfway down the market street when a brown tabby suddenly darted past us and just as quickly vanished into a narrow alley.

We followed the cat into the alley as if he were guiding us. The alley was just barely wide enough for a grown adult to walk down. Several children's bicycles had been left in the way, perhaps because there wasn't space for them in the houses that lined both sides. There was a concerning number of electric lines hanging from the telephone poles in a tangle overhead.

Megumi led the way. At the dead end, there was a rather old-looking building whose walls were covered in ivy. With its bungalow-style, A-frame roof on top and uniformly dark brown exterior, it looked more like a café than a home.

"Wait, there's a café all the way back here." Megumi forged ahead without waiting for my response, and snuck a peek at the interior through the glass door. "The inside looks nice too. Want to go in and check it out?"

We opened the door with the sign TORUNKA CAFÉ, and went inside.

As one might have expected from the outside, the interior of the café wasn't especially large. Aside from the seats at the counter, there were only five tables. Yet it was surprisingly crowded for a place that was so hard to find. All the tables were occupied except for one in the middle of the room.

Megumi quickly fell in love with the place and the way it felt so hidden away. After we were shown to our table, she started busily checking out everything inside, her gaze stopping first at the distinctive wooden mask on the wall—"I wonder if they bought that in Africa... That sleepy face kind of looks like you, Shūichi." She laughed. Her eyes were wide with excitement when she saw the classic pink pay phone in front of the bathroom, and she said, "That's incredible. They still have one of those!"

I was pretending to look around the café too, but I was secretly stealing glances at her as she sat there in front of me bubbling with childlike excitement. She smiles a lot, I thought. And the way she smiles is so natural, so unaffected.

That's when it hit me. I really am in love with this girl.

At that point in my life, I don't think I'd ever been in love before. Back at home, my parents ran a cocktail lounge together, but from my childhood on, their relationship was terrible. They only played at being a couple to keep up appearances and maintain the legal status of the lounge, but they each had younger lovers, and basically did whatever they wanted. Perhaps because I grew up watching my parents live like that, I had trouble understanding why people fell in love at all. I was always worried that I'd never be able to love someone.

But then I moved to Tokyo and met Megumi in college. She showed me that bright and carefree smile, and I said to myself maybe this is what it feels like to love someone. It meant so much to me—I was so happy I could have cried.

Even as we walked through the streets on the way home that night, the feelings that had welled up in me in the café showed no signs of fading. So I told Megumi how I truly felt about her—or rather, it might be more accurate to say the words came rushing out of me.

"I'm so happy. You finally said it." Then Megumi's face crumpled, and she looked as if she might laugh and cry at the same time. She laughed then, there in the street that night, overcome with emotion. "I've been waiting for this for a long time."

Not long after that, I happened to spot the notice saying they were looking for someone for a part-time position at the Torunka Café, and since I was looking for a job, I applied for it on the spot. I didn't even have a résumé with me, but the owner was kind enough to hire me.

Megumi often came as a customer, and would wait for me there to finish my shift. Shizuku and the owner used to tease us, saying, "Isn't it nice to be so happy together?" I was embarrassed, but Megumi would always laugh and say, "Yes, we are happy together."

But she'll probably never come back to the café. She'll never appear in the doorway out of breath and then sit drinking her coffee as she waits for me.

The old cliché might really be true: It's only after you lose something that you realize how precious it was. I learned it after I lost Megumi. I wish I could've spent my whole life without learning that lesson.

By the time I realized it, it was already the new year.

On the first Sunday at the end of break, Chinatsu Yukimura reappeared at the café.

Shizuku was away that day, so it was just the owner and me. That might have been a happy coincidence.

Because ever since that day at the end of the year, Shizuku had been trying relentlessly to get me to go out with Ms. Yukimura. "Come on, Shūichi," she'd say, "it's got to be fate."

That worried me, and I asked her if she actually believed it.

"It's strange, but it's nice to have dreams. I mean, being lovers during the French Revolution. And she's really cute. How old do you think she is? A little bit older than I am, right? You can pull it off. After all, you've got me in your corner!"

She was always egging me on like that. For some reason she was really taken with Chinatsu. Every time I saw her, she was always saying Chinatsu this and Chinatsu that. Maybe it was because Shizuku was a high school girl that she was into this kind of thing. It seems quite possible she just found the whole situation amusing.

The moment I realized Chinatsu Yukimura had come into the café, I immediately stiffened. Unlike last time, the café was pretty crowded, so there was no way I could handle it if things went the way they did last time. However, this time Chinatsu came up to me quite formally and bowed deeply.

"I apologize that I was so rude the other day."

"Uh, um, okay," I said, perplexed.

"I brought these for all of you to enjoy. I hope you don't mind."

She held out a box of desserts for me to take. Based on the wrapping paper, they seemed to be from the old traditional dessert shop on Yomise Street.

"Oh, thank you."

"Do you not like sweets?" she asked, afraid I might reject them.

"No, that's not it . . ."

"Oh, that's good, then."

A smile came to her face then, and she seemed relieved. Then she pulled her bangs forward as if she was trying to hide her eyes. It was apparently a habit of hers.

"Do you live around here?" the owner asked. He had been watching us from behind the counter with a huge smile on his face.

"Yes, just across from the station."

"Nicely done finding the place. Because of our location, people who don't live in the neighborhood tend not to notice us."

"There was this cat..."

She started to fidget and hesitate so much I was getting impatient.

"Hm?"

"The cat ran by and then I tried to chase after it..."

"Oh I see," the owner said, straining to smile.

"I'm sorry..."

"There's really no need to apologize."

As the owner got flustered, I was secretly struck by the fact that this was exactly what had happened to me. But of course I didn't let anyone see my reaction.

The always talkative Old Mr. Takita chose to butt in at that moment and started saying strange things. "What? A cat? You followed a cat here? That's just like in ... what do you call it? *Alice in the Valley of Wind.*"

The owner and I corrected him simultaneously: "*Alice in Wonderland.*" Besides, Alice wasn't chasing a cat; she was chasing a rabbit.

Anyway, after these brief hellos were over, Chinatsu sat down at the counter and quietly drank her coffee. She sat so still that from a distance you might have thought she was a figurine. And then, just like that, she got up and left with a quick bow.

Just as I was feeling a little bit disappointed that she'd simply gone home, the owner tapped me on the shoulder and said with a knowing smile, "She might be a little quiet, but she's cute, and she seems like a really nice girl, doesn't she? Besides, isn't it getting to be time to think about meeting someone new?"

I stared at him, wide-eyed with surprise. The owner, it seemed, had been worrying about me in his own way. Although it was also possible that, like his daughter, he simply found the whole thing amusing.

"But she is definitely a little . . ."

"I certainly don't believe in that past life stuff at all, but she's definitely not a bad person."

"How do you know that?"

"How many people do you think I've met working in this business? I can tell about a person once I've talked to them twice."

"That's super hard to believe," I said.

But the owner just gave a defiant little laugh.

From that day on, Chinatsu Yukimura came to the Torunka Café once a week without fail.

It was invariably on a Sunday, usually in the afternoon, a time when the café wasn't too busy. But when she came, she didn't seem to come with any particular purpose in mind.

She would always order her coffee and then stare off into space or read a book like *A Little Princess* or *The Secret Garden* or *Anne of Green Gables*, the kind of books that much younger girls tend to like. Sometimes our eyes would meet, and she'd smile shyly (when that happened, I'd have trouble keeping my composure). Then, after an hour or two, or, at the latest, when the sun went down, she would leave just as quietly as she'd come.

But don't be fooled. If the subject of our previous lives came up, she would change completely. Of course, I personally didn't want to hear another word about it. But the same can't be said for Shizuku, the Torunka Café's resident troublemaker. Although she had miraculously not been there when Chinatsu came the second time, now whenever Chinatsu appeared, Shizuku was always there waiting for a chance to sit down beside her and gleefully start up a conversation.

"It was the night right after we'd succeeded in storming the Bastille. All of us in the revolutionary army lit a fire in the square and drank wine together, reaffirming the comradery that bound us together."

"Oh, wow."

"Sylvie and I joined hands and stared into the bright red flames of the fire. We vowed then that once the battle was over we would get married. When I think of how beautiful Sylvie looked then, her face in profile lit by the roiling fire..."

I almost said, "I'm getting embarrassed just listening to this."

Every time I heard her talking in that dreamy way, I felt like I was about to get heartburn. She was like an adolescent girl, daydreaming about some fantasy—*if only it could be this way ... if only I met someone like that ...* As it escalated, I got the impression that she could no longer tell the difference between reality and these delusions.

Maybe it was time for her to leave all that behind.

"Um, hey."

Once they'd gotten used to going back and forth like that, I waited for the right moment to speak up. Looking back, I think it was the first time I started a conversation with her of my own accord.

"How old are you?"

"Me?"

"Yes."

I'd planned to gently persuade her that she couldn't just go on living in a dream, chasing butterflies through fields of flowers, but then ...

"I'm twenty-four," she said.

"Twenty-four ... Well, isn't it time for you to give up on these childish—wait, you're twenty-four?"

I flinched when I heard her actual age. I'd thought she was eighteen or nineteen. But she was three years older than I was, already a proper adult.

"Um, is something wrong?" Chinatsu looked at me with a puzzled expression on her face.

"No, it's just you're older than I am ..." I mumbled. It made me wonder even more if there was something wrong with her. Shizuku must've thought the same thing because she just sat there blinking.

"So, you have a job?"

"A job? Um, yes, I work at an automotive assembly plant."

"Chinatsu, you don't look all that strong though. Isn't it really difficult?" Shizuku spoke up, expressing the concerns I had precisely. I had trouble imagining her working in overalls, rather than in the kind of simple but cute dresses and blouses she liked to wear.

"It suits me better than using my brain at work. But I'm no good at it. I'm slow and I end up causing a lot of problems. I've been fired from two other places since I graduated high school. This is my third plant. I'm lucky they'll have me."

Without meaning to, I groaned in disbelief. Shizuku, who didn't seem to know how to respond either, just said, "Oh, that must be hard."

"No, no, I think it's harder on the people around me. I mean because of that, no one at the plant really speaks to me . . ."

"Does that mean," Shizuku asked in a whisper, "they're bullying you?"

"Hey!" I cut in, flustered. You can't ask that sort of thing so directly. You need to take a more roundabout approach. But Chinatsu didn't seem to mind.

"Bullied? No. It's not like that. They know that no matter how long I remain there, I'll never be of much use. I can see that I'm only causing problems, and I should just quit, but I need to make a living too."

"Chinatsu, would you like another cup of coffee?" I asked.

"Sorry?"

"I mean, I feel like having a cup, and while I'm at it, I thought . . . I'm just going to use the coffee beans I brought myself, so there's no need to pay."

She seemed at a loss, and I went in the back without waiting for a response. With the owner's permission, I made her a cup of the Colombian coffee she always ordered, and brought it to her shortly after.

Even I didn't quite understand why I'd done this.

It was partly because I didn't want to let the uneasy feeling in the room linger any longer. But that wasn't the only reason.

I was feeling a little embarrassed. I'd always been a lazy, obstinate person. I was always trying to avoid anything I saw as a hassle. I'd try to get by just talking my way out of things. And I'd been this way ever since I was a child. It's something I hated about myself. But now, confronted by someone like her, who was earnestly trying to make a life for herself, however ineptly, I was overwhelmed and I had to look away.

She was someone who'd worked much harder than I ever had. Regardless of whether she was a little odd, or whether she'd actually been my lover in a former life, she had more to be proud of than I, and she was far more resilient.

"It's delicious."

She gave a slight smile as she tasted the coffee I'd brought her. Then, naturally, she touched her bangs.

I quickly retreated to the kitchen again as though I hadn't heard what she said.

That evening, after Chinatsu Yukimura went home, as I was clearing her table, I heard Shizuku's voice from behind me, calling, "Hey, stop, stop!" and she rushed over to me, her ponytail swinging from side to side like the pendulum of a clock.

"What?"

She carefully picked up the small white object that had been left beside the coffee cup and held it up in front of me. "Look."

It wasn't much, just one of the café napkins folded in the figure of a ballerina.

"What about it?" I asked, without interrupting what I was doing. It might be rare, but it wasn't unheard of for customers to leave things on the tables. I couldn't understand why Shizuku would come running over to retrieve this particular thing.

"You don't get it?"

"Get what?"

"The ballerinas that Chinatsu makes are completely different from the ones other people make. Can't you tell these are incredibly good? She always leaves one for us."

Although I didn't think she was leaving them on purpose, I stared closely at the figure in the palm of Shizuku's hand. But I couldn't tell what was different about it. After all, whenever someone left something behind, I would throw it in the trash without paying much attention to it.

"What do you mean you can't see it, dummy? The ones Chinatsu makes are full of life. When you look at them, doesn't it seem like they have their own expressions? And the legs and arms are well balanced. Normally, people make the legs shorter, and the head bigger. They don't turn out this well."

Shizuku then turned to a regular customer who happened to be there, an older woman named Chiyoko, who was always knitting something, and held up the ballerina. "Chiyoko Bāchan, look at this!"

"Hey, that's quite good!" she exclaimed and started clapping. But Chiyoko was so nice I couldn't tell whether she was being sincere or just being polite.

"Oh, is it really so special?"

After my indifferent response, Shizuku got in a huff and said, "Okay, look here," and then, much to my irritation, she proceeded to force me to learn how to fold a ballerina from beginning to end. After folding the napkin into a narrow strip, you bring both ends together, then make a small incision. However, this proved fairly difficult for someone as obviously clumsy as I am.

Although I was somehow able to finish, the ballerina that emerged from my hands came out looking pretty terrible. She had thick, radish-shaped legs and short arms relative to the size of her head, and no waist—there was no way she was ever going to dance gracefully. Even still, it turned out so much worse than Chiyoko had expected that she doubled over laughing so hard that I worried she might die there on the spot.

"Um, it's definitely a lot harder than it looks," I reluctantly acknowledged.

"Right?" Shizuku huffed proudly, though it wasn't like she'd done it herself. Then, in a voice that was scarcely audible, she suddenly murmured, "I want Chinatsu to be happy..."

"You make it sound like she's totally unhappy now."

"Don't you..." She stopped then and looked down. But I understood what she meant.

It was precisely because I understood her that I felt uneasy.

Shizuku might have seemed like a cheerful girl, but she was much more delicate than she looked. A single word or gesture could have such an impact on her that she'd end up feeling hurt on someone else's behalf. A sad news story on television was enough to make her depressed. She was a kind, good-hearted girl, but I'd sometimes watch her and worry.

I tried patting her on the head where her long hair was pulled back in a ponytail. I was acting like a guy in a teen drama, cheering up the heroine. But she immediately pushed my hand away. I should've seen that coming.

"I've been thinking for a while now that you've really got a soft spot for her, Shizuku."

"Hmmm..." Shizuku thought for a moment and then suddenly smiled. "Maybe a little. She reminds me of someone I know."

"Really?"

"Yeah, maybe it's her taste in clothes, the way she likes to read. There's just something about her that reminds me of someone. When I talk to Chinatsu, it makes me kind of nostalgic."

The narrow eyes she'd inherited from her father grew narrower as if she was remembering something.

"Chinatsu loves the Torunka Café too. She told me that coming here calms her down, and makes her feel ready to face the days to come. Sundays are her day off, you know. And she spends that precious day with us. When you think about that, doesn't it make you so happy you could cry?"

Her smile then was of a completely different nature from her usual smile at work. From behind the counter, she took out a tin that once held an assortment of cookies. She started to put the ballerina Chinatsu had made inside it.

"You mean you've been saving them?"

"I've picked up all the ones I noticed. From now on, Shūichi, you can't throw them away," Shizuku said and then showed me the contents of the tin. Inside it, there were already three ballerinas.

"Wouldn't it be wonderful if I joined their hands together and made a sort of lace archway from one end of the counter to the other?"

"Really?" I looked back at her a little confused. I didn't get it.

But Shizuku said, "Really!" in such a menacing way that I knew I had no choice but to agree with her.

"It looks like you're still a long way from having enough to make an arch."

I guessed it would take at least thirty to reach both ends of the counter. No, maybe fifty. How many Sundays would it take? If she wanted that many, she could just come out and ask Chinatsu, and she'd make her a whole stack of them. But when I brought up the idea, Shizuku just said, "Where's the fun in that? So we need Chinatsu to keep coming for a long time," Shizuku said, laughing a little to herself again.

I thought the warm days would continue in February, but the following night there were snow flurries, and the fierce cold returned.

My poorly constructed window clattered loudly with every gust of wind. Cold air poured mercilessly through the gaps. I could still see my breath inside my apartment. I thought about how often Megumi would come to visit me there.

The day before I'd bumped into her at the entrance to the school cafeteria for the first time in a long while. I'd let my guard down because there weren't many people coming to campus now that the miserable days of final exams were over. Since our breakup, I'd been doing my best to avoid seeing her.

There was a brief awkward moment at first, but then Megumi gave her usual smile and said, "It's been so long. How are you doing?"

"I'm okay. How about you?"

"I'm okay."

"Oh."

That's all we said to each other, then we quickly waved goodbye and went our separate ways.

It's strange, but although I still couldn't get Megumi out of my mind, I sincerely hoped she was happy now on her own. I said to myself I'm glad she seems like she's doing well. And yet, her leaving me had left a little hole in my heart that I could never fill, and I knew that the pain it left behind would never go away.

"Hey Sylvie, time to take Chinatsu home!"

One Sunday evening, I was just getting ready to leave the café and go home, when Shizuku called out to stop me. It was already five, the end of my shift, and Chinatsu was uncustomarily still at the Torunka Café.

"Sylvie who?" I tried to scowl at Shizuku, but she brushed me off.

"It's already pretty dark outside. Things might have been reversed in your previous life, but in this one, Chinatsu is a girl, so..."

"No, no, please, I don't want to impose!" Chinatsu said, looking flustered as she stood up, but Shizuku overruled her.

"Now, now," she said, taking a tight grip of my sleeve as I tried to get away. "It's not a problem, is it?"

I could tell from her voice that I had no other option, so I reluctantly agreed. After what had happened with Megumi, I really wasn't in a good mood, but I figured I could handle this much.

"Well, I'm going to cut across the market street and head to the train station. Shall we go together?"

"Are you sure you don't mind?"

"It's on my way anyway," I said nonchalantly.

Chinatsu got up and hurried to try to put her coat on. "Okay, then, sure. Let's go!"

"You don't have to rush. I can wait."

"No, now's perfect!" she said, although her bag was wide open, giving me a full view of its contents, and she still hadn't paid her bill. When I pointed this out, she turned red and handed her money to Shizuku. Watching this chain of events unfold was too much for me, and I burst out laughing. Chinatsu stood there staring at me, blinking. "Yes?"

"Okay, let's go," I said, playing dumb.

"Okay!" she said as cheerfully as a dog happy to be taken on a walk.

I led the way, as we went down Torunka Street (that's the name Shizuku had taken the liberty of giving to the little alley the café was on) and came out onto the market street.

It was near sunset, and the streetlights of Yanaka Ginza were already giving off a pale white glow. The street was full of housewives looking for ingredients for dinner that night as cheerful music played from the speakers overhead. We crossed the street in front of the butcher shop, and as the scent of meat drifted our way, my stomach grumbled loudly, demanding a sacrificial offering.

I was walking with my hands shoved into the pockets of the army coat I'd bought for 1,950 yen as part of my strategy to get through this year's winter. Chinatsu was walking beside me, with her face buried in the same bright scarlet scarf she was wearing the first time we'd met. The cold winter wind blew through us, gently ruffling her shoulder-length hair.

It occurred to me at that moment that this was the first time I'd been with her outside the café. All in all, we'd known each other for two months. My initial resistance had gone away somehow. Yet I definitely wasn't ready to think of her as someone I might go out with, the way the owner and his daughter had been pushing me to.

Be that as it may, my choice to walk home by going down the market street was extremely foolish.

We immediately came to the attention of the man who ran the fruit and vegetable stand, who also just happened to be a regular at the café. He called over to us, "Oh hey, it's the guy from the café. Out on a date tonight?"

Soon we could hear them talking at the delicatessen and the tea house across the street. "Oooh, he's on a date!" "Hey, it's good to be young, isn't it?"

I had no choice but to deny everything.

At some point, I'd become someone people in the neighborhood knew by sight. They were all surprisingly open and friendly, so I should have expected that something like this might happen. I kept walking, feeling an indescribable discomfort. But next to me, Chinatsu showed no signs of being particularly embarrassed, maybe because she hadn't noticed that they were actually teasing me.

When we'd finally gotten away from the banter, Chinatsu smiled and said, "Shūichi, you still rub your ear whenever you don't know what to do. Just like you used to." I was shocked. She said it like she'd genuinely known me for a long time. But was this really about a previous life? "Oh boy," I said with a pained laugh.

"I'm sorry. That sounded weird," she said.

"Don't worry about it."

She was looking at me with a surprisingly happy expression on her face.

"There are so many delightful people in this neighborhood," she said.

"Delightful?" I had to laugh. It seemed a little off the mark. "Well, they're friendly, I guess. There are all kinds of neighborhoods in Tokyo. It's not like that back where I'm from."

She turned to me and said, "Where are you from?"

"Oh yeah, I'm from Wakayama. We used to live near the city though, so we didn't have especially close relationships with people there."

She was still staring at me intently. A mother and her son crossed in front of us, chanting, "Poopie poop poop," and I took hold of Chinatsu's arm and pulled her back so she didn't run into them.

"Oh, I'm sorry," she said.

"Is something wrong?"

"What?"

"You were so focused on what I was saying," I said.

"I'm just really interested."

"In where I'm from?"

I supposed she was simply interested in getting to know me. Up to that point, though, she hadn't really asked me about myself. But now, instead of answering my question, she asked another. "Shūichi, why did you come to Tokyo?"

"Oh, um, because I wanted to go to college here."

Although I'd given a simple answer, she kept looking at me like she was waiting for me to say more.

"My parents were pretty terrible. Especially my father. When the place he ran turned out to be a big hit and he was raking it in, he lived a wild, debauched life. It started when I was a child. I wanted to get away from all of that. He was the kind of parent who dragged his clueless kid along with him when he went to his girlfriend's place. I guess he figured that he could fool my mom if I went with him. And he made me wait outside the whole time he was getting it on with the woman. It didn't matter if it was the middle of summer and the sun was beating down on me."

I laughed as I remembered those days and felt the bitterness welling up in me. I found myself daydreaming for a moment, wondering what would've happened if I'd been born near here, in the warmth of this neighborhood of little shops and markets, surrounded by all these kind people—maybe I wouldn't have turned out so messed up.

"His girlfriend's run-down house looked like it had been forgotten by everyone else, and the others nearby were all the same. It was really desolate. We happened to be well off then, but whenever he brought me there, I'd think to myself, wow, there are places like this too. I remember feeling sad without quite knowing why."

Thinking back on that period of my life that I'd almost entirely forgotten put me in a bit of a dark mood. I was that kid again, standing there on that lonesome road, with the heat of the sun slowly roasting the back of my neck. The hopelessness, not knowing what to do with myself. All I could do was wait for my father to come back.

"Well, it's not like I had to go to Tokyo in particular. I just wanted to leave home. And without me there, my father and my mother were free to do as they wished, so they were only too happy to let me go."

But right after I moved to Tokyo, the lounge my father ran started to go under, and now it was a sinking ship. Given how carelessly he'd managed the place, it shouldn't have come as a surprise. You could even argue it was long overdue. I bore the brunt of repercussions. It was looking like I might have to get another part-time job to pay for my tuition and living expenses this semester.

I realized then that Chinatsu was looking at me with a pained expression, like she felt sorry for me.

"Forgive me. That must've sounded strange," I said, but Chinatsu shook her head, flustered. I must have been out of my mind to tell her all that.

Chinatsu didn't say anything else for a long while, but once we could see the entrance to Nippori Station, she suddenly spoke up. "Um, Shūichi . . . No, it's nothing . . . I'm sorry. I'm sorry I brought back such sad memories."

"Forget about it. I'm the one who brought it up. I've been kind of down recently and sometimes I ramble."

She stared at me again and seemed to be searching for the right words to say. She was looking right at me with these beautiful eyes. I felt my chest grow warm and quickly looked away.

"I'm, um, I'm glad we met, Shūichi. I really am. It's not just about our previous lives . . . I really want to thank you."

"You don't have to thank me."

Then, all of a sudden, she cried out in a shrill voice, "Let's keep going with zero accidents!"

"What?"

"At my job, we all have to say that at the end of our morning assembly. It means let's go another day without any accidents. The other people don't seem to like saying it, but I really do enjoy saying it in the morning. It's like a good luck charm. It lifts my spirits and makes me feel ready to do my best."

"I see." In my head, I was thinking, What? but, after a moment or two, somehow I started to understand what she meant. She probably thought I was feeling down and just wanted to cheer me up.

"Shūichi, you can say it too if you want."

"Me?"

We were in front of the station, so there were a fair number of people around us. And now because Chinatsu had just been shouting, some people were looking at us. How was I supposed to shout in a place like that? But Chinatsu was still watching me earnestly.

"Um... Let's keep going with zero accidents...?"

"Could you maybe say it a little louder for me?"

"Let's keep going with zero accidents!" I screamed madly. The salaryman who happened to be passing right in front of us at that moment jumped back and gave us a puzzled look. When a guy suddenly screams like that in the middle of the city in winter, people are going to be surprised.

"That's wonderful. How do you feel? Don't you feel a little better?"

She asked me the question so earnestly that I couldn't say I was merely embarrassed. I felt a strange sense of peace, perhaps just from shouting out loud, regardless of the meaning of the words themselves. It reminded me that I rarely ever raise my voice. It always seemed like more trouble than it was worth.

I realized I was smiling. "Yeah," I said, "I think so."

"I'm glad to hear that." She let out a big sigh like she'd just accomplished something important. "Well, this is it for me," she said, and before I knew it, she'd gone off and left me alone in front of the station.

I felt the chilly wind nipping at my nose as I stood there in a daze, watching her walking away. Then I sneezed.

One afternoon only a few days later, I showed up to work at the Torunka Café on my way home from campus and saw a tall teenager standing out front.

It was Kōta, a high school student who lived in the neighborhood. He looked like he was on his way home from school because he was wearing his navy-blue uniform blazer.

"What are you doing?"

When I called out to him, he turned around and gave me a quick bow. "Oh, hey."

Kōta seemed like a bright, easygoing guy, the kind who's the life of the party in high school. I'm sure he was a pretty naughty kid when he was little. Even though he was in his sophomore year of high school now, the women in the neighborhood still called him the little troublemaker.

"So what are you doing?"

"I'm waiting for Shizuku. She doesn't seem to be coming out though."

"Shizuku? Is there some special reason you're waiting in front of the café for her?"

"Some special reason? Don't you know what day it is?" Kōta pressed me for an answer with an exasperated look on his face.

"What do you mean? What is it?"

"The fourteenth! It's Valentine's Day. How do you not know that? Is there something wrong with your head?"

When I finally got it, I said, "Oh, so that's why you're waiting for Shizuku."

Shizuku and Kōta were childhood friends, having been in school together from kindergarten through high school. On top of that, Kōta had had a crush on Shizuku since they were children. Which was why you'd often see him getting bossed around by her.

"Shūichi, you're not into it?"

"Valentine's Day? Honestly, I'm not really interested in that sort of thing. The whole idea of a woman giving chocolates to a man she's got her eye on was started as a scheme by the candy companies anyway."

"A scheme? You're not much of a romantic, are you? Shizuku was telling me you've been living a quiet life these days."

"Is that right?"

"Yeah, maybe you're losing your youthful vigor. You ought to eat more meat."

"You sure those two things are connected?"

As we were discussing the issue, Shizuku came out wearing an apron over her school uniform.

"Hey," she said haughtily, and held out what looked like a gift box with a flashy wrapping paper that she'd bought in the neighborhood. Kōta accepted it meekly. After inspecting it closely, he nodded and said, "I graciously accept the fruits of your love." Then, ignoring Shizuku's reply—"It's definitely not love!"—he bid us farewell and walked off toward the shopping.

So much for romance, I guess. Maybe that's how it goes when you've been friends since childhood.

I walked into the café, already warmed by the heater, muttering under my breath, "Talk about not being romantic."

"If I don't give him anything, he sulks. It's annoying. He's held it against me for three years. You see, when I was in my second year of middle school, I forgot to give him a gift—he's still complaining about it," Shizuku said coldly, casually scratching the thigh that was jutting out from the pleated skirt of her school uniform.

"Shizuku, what if you quit worrying about other people's love affairs and give thought to your own situation?"

"I'm not interested in stuff like that. I'm busy with the café, and I've got chores to do too."

Because of what was going on with Shizuku's family, she and the owner were living alone together (I'd heard her mom was living abroad). So, she was the one bearing the responsibility for taking care of things at home. She was actually kind of an amazing kid, even if she still seemed pretty childish and wouldn't touch coffee.

"More importantly though, Chinatsu's got to be coming today, right?"

"Why? It's not Sunday."

"Oh, come on, it's obvious. She's going to bring you chocolates. And they're definitely going to be homemade. Chinatsu seems good at that sort of thing. She's got to be a great cook."

The thought hadn't even crossed my mind until Shizuku brought it up. Chinatsu and I weren't young sweethearts, afraid to express our feelings. I was sure Shizuku was wrong. But it caught me so off guard that my voice cracked when I tried to respond. "You can't just leap to a conclusion like that."

"There's no doubt about it. She's crazy about you," Shizuku said, brimming with confidence.

A moment ago when I'd told Kōta I had zero interest in Valentine's Day, I wasn't making excuses for myself for not being able to find a girlfriend. I just never got into the idea of Valentine's Day. I suppose because ever since I was a child, I've always been pretty disillusioned about that sort of thing.

Yet, after Shizuku declared that Chinatsu was in love with me, I found myself struggling to regain my composure. I started imagining Chinatsu coming to give me her homemade chocolates. She'd smile shyly. Her cheeks would blush, and she'd fiddle with her bangs.

The image calmed me down. It was like I was a child again staring at the pages of my favorite picture book.

"Hey, Sylvie, you're looking forward to it, aren't you?" Shizuku said with a dirty little smirk on her face, like she could tell what I was thinking.

"Sylvie who? I'm not looking forward to anything."

"Oh, you don't have to hide it. Why should you? I've been rooting for Chinatsu this whole time. I'm happy you've got a crush on her now."

"I don't have a crush." I denied it right away, but Shizuku just ignored me and said, "Sure, sure."

And yet Chinatsu still didn't show up.

At sunset, as evening set in, the bell on the door chimed, but she wasn't the one who walked in. Sunset comes so early in winter, I thought to myself. The sky turns black without mercy. I went about my job acting as if nothing were happening, but inside I was on pins and needles. And it was all because of what Shizuku had said. In my heart, I was cursing the poster girl of the Torunka Café.

Sometime after six, the door was flung open and I heard a young woman's voice calling hello. Shizuku and I turned and looked at the same time.

"Ugh, is that Ayako?" Shizuku said, making absolutely no attempt to disguise her disappointment. Ayako lived nearby and worked at the flower shop on the market street. Among the Torunka Café's predominantly middle-aged and senior citizen clientele, she was a rare and precious thing: a young regular customer. She was a funny and openhearted girl, but unfortunately she wasn't the person we were waiting for.

"Um, what's going with you two? You don't want me to be here?"

"He's the one to ask." Shizuku was trying to lay the blame on me.

"No, no, that's not it at all." I shook my head, flustered.

"What's going on? You two are acting weird. Don't you know the saying 'Knock and the door shall be opened unto you'?"

"Nope," we said at the same time.

Ayako had a habit of writing down great quotes and keeping them in her notebook. She would recite one whenever she got the chance. She considered herself a quote fanatic, and obviously had amassed considerable knowledge in this area, but I got the feeling there was sometimes something a little off in the way she used them.

"That's cold, especially since I came all this way in the snow."

"Wait, it's snowing?" I shouted, surprised by Ayako's announcement.

"Just a little at the moment, but it looks like it's going to snow through the night."

When I opened the window and looked outside at Torunka Street, I saw Ayako was right. It wasn't coming down hard enough to accumulate, but snowflakes were fluttering down from the sky, white against the dark night. She won't come, I thought. There's no reason to expect her now.

While I was feeling dejected, Ayako brought out another one of her funny quotes. "Ooh, it's cold out there," she said. "I'm going to drink my coffee and hurry home. After all, 'to live is not merely to breathe but to take action,' you know?"

Finally, it was past nine o'clock, closing time. The snow was still coming down outside the windows.

"She didn't come, I guess."

Even Shizuku had to admit that she wasn't coming, but as we got the café ready to close, she still didn't seem entirely convinced.

"Cheer up. She probably just got busy at work. Or maybe, because your roles were reversed in your previous life, and you were the woman and she was the man, she was waiting on the edge of her seat for you to give her chocolate."

Maybe she was right. Should I have brought Chinatsu chocolates instead? In that case, I could go out first thing tomorrow morning and buy some . . . No, that can't be it. On Valentine's Day, women give men chocolate. White Day is the other way around. Why would she mix those up? I must be so tired from waiting all day that it's affecting my brain, and I'm starting to believe in Shizuku's absurd reasoning.

At that moment, we heard the jingling of the bell on the door. "Can I still come in?"

My heart just about stopped. I saw a hand holding a light blue umbrella appear behind the door, and the face that peeked out from underneath it, short of breath, belonged to the person I'd been waiting for all day. It was unmistakably Chinatsu Yukimura herself. As soon as Shizuku recognized her, she got so ridiculously excited that she started shouting like a fisherman who'd just hooked a big one.

"Oh, Chinatsu, what's wrong?" The owner, who had managed to go all day without noticing it was Valentine's Day, popped his head out from behind the counter and spoke to Chinatsu.

"I'm sorry. I'll leave right away, but is it all right if I come in for a moment?" she asked apologetically.

"No objection from me, but . . ." the owner said, though he seemed mystified.

"Oh, thank you. Um, Shūichi . . ." she said, and turned to me and hurried over to me, half running. It looked as if she might have run here in the snow because her elegantly cut hair was all tangled. White snowflakes were glistening as they melted on her shoulders and in her black hair. I couldn't look away. In the orange light of the lanterns, the melting snow was as beautiful as jewels.

"I had to stay late at work, but here, it's, um, chocolate, if that's okay..." Chinatsu nervously held out a paper bag for me to take, almost like a child who was afraid of being scolded.

"Oh, thank you." I noticed then that I was rubbing my ear without meaning to. Just as she'd pointed out before, it's a habit I've had for forever. I do it whenever I'm embarrassed. Which meant that she knew full well that I was embarrassed at that moment. But I didn't need to worry about that, because she seemed to be in her own world, nervously tugging on her bangs.

"I made the chocolates this morning, but they didn't turn out. They didn't keep their shape. If they don't taste good, please don't feel bad about throwing them away."

"No, no, I'll eat them. Thank you very much." When I expressed my sincere gratitude, Chinatsu's cheeks turned so red it was funny. To hide it, she pulled on her bangs so hard that I worried she might yank them out.

Contrary to what I'd imagined, even seeing Chinatsu arrive, chocolate in hand, didn't bring me any peace. I felt overcome by even more anxiety. Her slender hand that was touching her hair looked cold. I wanted to hold it and warm it in mine.

I glanced over and saw Shizuku nodding and looking as if at any moment she might announce, "I knew this would happen."

These minor events piled up, accumulating like the snow that fell that night, and by the time the end of winter had rolled around, our relationship had definitively changed. It was hard to believe that we'd only met right before New Year's.

Before I knew it, we'd gotten into the habit of leaving together on Sundays.

I say "together," but we really only went as far as the train station. It wasn't a big deal. We only exchanged a few words here and there along the way.

One Sunday, she spoke passionately about how much she loved the character of Matthew, the adoptive father in *Anne of Green Gables*, one of her favorite books.

"Matthew is shy and hardworking and kind. He looks out for her, like he'll always be there to protect her. He's the kind of person you can't help but love."

I'm not sure I could say I was familiar with the character of Matthew, but I got a good sense of how much she loved him.

On another Sunday, I taught her how to spot stray cats because I knew how much she liked them. She turned to some cats sitting on a fence and the shed of someone's home, glaring gloomily back at us, and gave them a sincere bow and said, "Nice to meet you." I burst out laughing.

As one Sunday followed the next, I learned more and more about her. It might seem to most people that it took frustratingly long for us to get to know each other. There are certainly far simpler ways for two people to bridge the distance between them. But for us—well, for me at least—it felt right.

From everything I learned, Chinatsu Yukimura was serious, humble, and a little awkward. She had absolutely no ill intentions toward anyone. She never said an unkind word about anyone, and never judged things from a merely one-sided point of view.

Being with her made me feel like I could be a better person too. When we were together, I felt like I could be at peace with the world. I was always looking askew at the world, but she was the opposite, she looked straight at it with clear eyes. It honestly made me jealous of her, but I thought it was wonderful.

As my feelings for Chinatsu grew stronger, I felt my attachment to Megumi become more and more a memory. Megumi was now my ex-girlfriend, but I felt a gentle pang in my heart from time to time when I thought about our relationship.

With this new beginning, something else was quietly coming to an end. All through the end of winter, I had a hunch that both happiness and sadness were coming my way.

And yet ...

Sometime after the middle of March, Shizuku surprised me by telling me that she was worried.

"Hey, Shūichi, you didn't say anything weird to Chinatsu, did you? When she was here last week, she seemed kind of down, don't you think?"

I could hardly believe my ears. I'd honestly thought things were going well between us. She hadn't said much, but she was always quiet, so I didn't notice anything different.

"I mean, she didn't even want to talk about Sylvie and Etienne."

"Personally, I thought that was a good thing," I said with a laugh, thinking that Shizuku was still holding on to her first impression of Chinatsu. That was just her imagination getting a little out of hand. I'd already sorted it out in my mind.

If she hadn't mentioned it, it was only because she no longer needed that nonsense to get my attention.

"Um ..."

My explanation did not seem to satisfy Shizuku.

"It's not just that. She just seemed depressed somehow. It felt like she was brooding over something. That's why I thought you must have said something."

I shook my head. To tell the truth, I was planning on asking her out next week.

That's right. As slow as I am, I'd finally decided that it was time to take the next step. Or rather, to be honest, I'd realized that the little bit of time I spent with her on Sundays was no longer enough. So I made a plan to use White Day as an excuse to invite her out. But I was still only at the planning stages. I hadn't said a word about it.

"Is that right? I guess things are okay, then."

At last, Shizuku was persuaded it might just have been her imagination. Then we changed the subject, and I stopped thinking about it and completely forgot about the whole thing.

The next Sunday, I felt a little more anxious than usual. So, as soon as we had gone out from the Torunka Street to the market street, I went right ahead and asked her out without even pausing to get a sense of how she seemed.

"Why don't we go out sometime?"

But the look on her face was the opposite of what I'd expected. She was clearly uncomfortable.

"Oh, that's, um . . ." Chinatsu looked down and fidgeted nervously. I wouldn't have minded at all if she was just being shy, but that wasn't what was happening. She was troubled.

"I'm sorry if I made you uncomfortable," I said, flustered.

"No, it's not that at all." But after she said that she seemed unable to say more.

Outwardly, I kept calm, but inside I was a complete mess. Given the relationship we'd developed so far, I'd had complete confidence. I never imagined she might react this way.

"I wanted to thank you for the chocolates, but . . ."

"The chocolates? Oh, um, I just forced those on you. It was my selfish way of thanking you for how nice you always are to me. There's no need to thank me..."

Her vague answer only left me more discouraged. What I'd thought of as a dramatic turn of events, she was now referring to as her own selfish act. What the hell was going on? All the excitement I'd been feeling suddenly disappeared.

We remained that way as we climbed the slope of Gotenzaka together, reaching the station without saying a word. After a vague goodbye, we went our separate ways, leaving an awkward silence between us.

I ended up spending the next week mulling over my massive disappointment and regrets.

What had I done wrong?

Why had she reacted so strangely?

No matter how much I thought it over, I couldn't figure it out.

There was just no explanation. From the outside, there was nothing wrong with our relationship. But the moment I tried to get closer to her, she pushed me away.

What on earth had happened?

I spent days in anguish over these questions until the next Sunday arrived.

I had no idea what to say on the way home.

Despite what had happened the week before, Chinatsu Yukimura showed up that Sunday the way she always did, and when it got dark, she got up from her chair as usual, and the two of us left together. Then we walked along the market street the way we always did, feeling rather uneasy (or at least that's how I felt).

"Um, Shūichi..."

We'd made it to the end of the market street and reached the little staircase known as the Sunset Steps when Chinatsu, who had been silent the whole way, suddenly said my name.

"Do you have a few minutes? There's something I want to tell you." Chinatsu hung her head down and gripped the straps of her bag so tightly that her fingertips turned red.

"What is it . . . ?" I asked, unable to hide the tremble in my voice. I sounded shrill. I had absolutely no idea what she was going to tell me. The only thing she made clear was that it was something important. And without a doubt, it was not going to be the sort of talk that would leave me a happier man.

Lit up by the setting sun, Chinatsu stood there with her lips held tight, staring down at the shadow she cast on the concrete, as she seemed to wonder how to broach the subject. Everything was at peace on the market street. The same cheerful music was playing on the speakers the way it always did.

But the grave expression on Chinatsu's face was completely at odds with all that.

"Sure," I said. "Let's go someplace where it will be easier to talk."

"Thank you."

She walked in front and led us to a little park not far ahead, a very tiny little park with only a poor excuse for a slide and a swing. It was still light outside, but streetlights inside the park were shining. In less than thirty minutes, we would be surrounded by darkness.

I followed a step behind Chinatsu as she led the way to a bench beside the swing set. Luckily, we'd reached the season where it wasn't too cold to be outside at this time of day.

"Are you cold?"

"I'm fine," Chinatsu said in a quiet voice when she finally looked up. "I'm sorry. I'm always, always imposing on you. To think that I even pushed you to consider asking me out..."

Pushed me? Is that how she saw it? That was too much. When I let my shoulders droop in disappointment, she said something that surprised me even more.

"But this is going to be the last time..."

"What do you mean the last time?"

I found myself shouting far too loudly for this quiet little park.

"Once you hear what I have to say, you probably won't want to see me ever again. That's why I've decided that today is the last time I'll ever go to the Torunka Café."

Why would she feel the need to do something so drastic? Was she keeping some dark secret from me? But it didn't seem like we'd gotten close enough yet for her to have that kind of secret.

"I lied to you," she said, focusing all her attention on her hands, which were gripping her legs tightly just above her knees.

"You lied?"

"Yes, about meeting you in a previous life."

The heaviness in the air was immediately forgotten, and I felt like I might burst out laughing. If that's all it was, I'd known that for a while. What was more worrying to me was the idea that she might not be aware it was a lie. I was on the verge of feeling at ease when Chinatsu said something unexpected. "That was wrong. Though it's true that we had met before. I kept telling myself that I had to say this to you, but I didn't have the courage, so I ended up putting it off for so long. I'm truly sorry."

"I'm afraid I don't understand."

"You and I actually met when we were children."

"Huh?" I automatically searched Chinatsu's face for some kind of clue. She lifted her head and looked back at me. The sun was already setting, and her face was made strangely white by the glow of the streetlight. In the distance, a dog gave a short bark.

"Shūichi, you told me about it yourself. How your father would often take you with him to that woman's house."

"Oh, yes, I guess . . ."

"I was there too."

"You?"

"Yes, how much do you remember from those days?"

"Not that much, I suppose. I just remember that he used to take me to that house a lot."

I guess I must have been around four years old then. I knew deep down that I'd experienced those things, but there's no way I could remember all the details.

"Is that right . . . You were a lot younger than me, and I'm sure you don't want to remember what happened. That would be perfectly natural. But I was there. That woman was my mother."

I stared at her, dumbfounded. It was impossible to believe. How could it be true? Could Chinatsu be the daughter of my father's lover? But the two of us had just met by chance in Tokyo not that long ago. Then Chinatsu said that wasn't actually what happened.

"It wasn't by chance. I've been looking for you for a long time."

"What? Why?" I said, unable to hide my confusion.

"I just wanted to see you," she replied without hesitation.

She prefaced what followed by saying, "It's kind of a long story. I hope it's okay," and then began to falter as she went on. "My mother, I must say as her daughter, was a very loose woman. She wasn't always like that. But after she and my father got divorced, her life changed completely. She drew a lot of men to that house. And if they didn't seem to love her, she would get so anxious she couldn't bear it. When I think about it now, I see she was suffering from mental illness.

"You might not remember those days, Shūichi, but I do. Your father often brought you by the hand to the house where my mother and I lived. When my mother invited your father inside, she ordered me to wait outside with you. I was a terribly shy child, and I couldn't really open up to you right away. But when I looked at you standing there, on the verge of tears, I couldn't take it. I gathered my courage and made an effort to get close to you. I guess it worked because little by little we started to become friends.

"You were already an extremely cute little boy. I even caught myself thinking that this is what it would be like if I had a little brother. The idea tickled me. The two of us used to draw pictures with chalk on the street in front of my house, and go out exploring the drainage ditch nearby. And you were always toddling along behind me. I told myself I was like your older sister, so I decided on my own that I had to be the one to protect you.

"In those days, I was a hopeless dreamer. I loved reading, and it would leave me lost in daydreams, to the point that I'd end up feeling like the stories had happened to me in real life. Like my father was a multimillionaire who had to follow his job and work abroad, but he'd be coming home soon to see me . . . or like there was a secret tunnel in our garden and it led to another world . . . I told you one of those stories once when you got so tired of waiting for your father that you started crying, and it seemed like you really liked it. After that, you were always pestering me to tell you a story. I got so into it that every night when I went to bed I would spend every moment I could thinking of one story after another that I could tell you the next time I saw you. It's stupid, but it made me so happy to see you smile..."

She glanced at me, then laughed for a moment and smiled gently. A soft breeze blew across her face, ruffling her bangs.

I realized then that she'd shown me that warm, gentle smile many times before.

It was like she could see inside me to the little boy I once was. But the smile only appeared for a moment before it vanished from her face.

"My mother looked at me and said, 'You've really taken a liking to that kid, haven't you?' She laughed. Then she said, 'It might not be that long before he really is your little brother.' When I heard that, I couldn't contain my excitement. It seemed so wonderful. Having a new father and a new little brother would be the start of a wonderful life—just the thought was enough to make me feel like running outside and dancing in the street."

Another gentle breeze made her bangs flutter again.

"But after the end of fall that year, your father suddenly stopped coming. And that meant, Shūichi, that you never came again. I casually asked my mother about it once, but she flew into a violent rage. After that, she didn't speak about it anymore, and I stopped asking."

When she reached that point in her story, Chinatsu stopped for a moment and said nothing. Then she exhaled, only a little, but her chest seemed terribly heavy.

It was only the two of us in the park now. All around us it was quiet. The stars were shining dimly in the night sky. We could hear the sound of cars driving past in the distance, a faint, low buzzing in our ears. Farther away, the dog barked again for a moment.

"That's all . . . true, isn't it?" I couldn't help asking her to reassure me.

"It is. It's all true. I swear."

"It's true?" I ransacked my memory, trying to recall that period in my life. But I couldn't. I felt certain that I used to talk to another child there who was close to my age. And I felt certain it was a girl. But beyond that, I was at a loss. It was that those memories had been sealed away, and all I could recall were hazy scenes.

I felt myself slipping into a dark mood. The story she had told—assuming it was all true—was painful for me too. Because, in the end, it was all my father's fault. How did she feel when after hoping and dreaming of beginning a new family with her mother, she was betrayed by my father? How disappointed must she have felt? How could my father have behaved so terribly?

Maybe she could tell what I was feeling because Chinatsu quietly shook her head.

"Your father wasn't the only one at fault. I think my mother had her own selfish motives. After all, your father wasn't the only one visiting us. And I think I knew in my heart from the beginning that it was never going to turn out well. My mother was just a weak person."

I could only nod vaguely without saying anything.

"Then, the year before last, long after those days, after my mother had been ill in body and mind for many years, when we knew at last that she did not have much time left, I asked her again about your father. I knew that if I didn't ask then, I wouldn't get another chance. My mother laughed. 'You really want to know about something from so long ago?' But she answered my question. She told me about how she had been working at the place your father ran and how they gradually fell into a relationship.

"One night, I went to the place my mother had told me about. I only wanted to know one thing: whether you were okay now. That's all. I explained to your father that I was an old friend of yours, and I asked him what you were up to now. That's how I learned that you were in Tokyo, working at a café in a place called Yanaka. When I heard that, I knew deep down that I had done the right thing, summoning all my courage to visit your father. Because now I knew that the boy I'd been worried about all this time was doing fine, even if it was in a faraway city."

"Does that mean," I interjected, "that you came to Tokyo to see me?"

Chinatsu reached her hand up to touch her bangs and she nodded. "I guess that could be true," she mumbled.

"I didn't even consider the idea at first. But, like I was saying earlier, my mother passed away around then. At which point, I realized something that surprised me. That there was no longer any reason for me to remain where I was. I suddenly thought about going to see Tokyo. And you were here. When I look back on my life, I really don't have many memories that make me truly smile like that. That period of my life is a really precious memory.

"I can't tell you how much strength those memories gave me when things got hard . . . It's not like I thought deeply about it all. But before I knew it, my mind was made up. At the time it seemed like if I came here, things might change . . ."

After that, she said, she came to Tokyo all by herself, bringing almost nothing with her. As luck would have it, she found a place to work at a new factory in the area. This was a little less than a year ago, she said.

"On Sundays, which were my day off from work, I would walk around the neighborhood. To be honest, I didn't have much hope that we'd see each other again. As I learned once I got to Tokyo, there are a lot of cafés in the neighborhood, and since the only clue I had was that it was in Yanaka, it didn't seem like I had a great chance of finding you. And there was no guarantee that you were still working here. Still, I walked the neighborhood on my days off, and whenever I found a new place, I always went in. I kept it up for a year, and over time my plan to find you faded, and it became just my routine. But then, at the end of last year, by chance, and I mean truly by chance, I found the Torunka Café..."

She stopped at that point, and glanced at me. When her eyes met mine, she looked down again.

"I came in, but I didn't realize it was you right away. When you think about it, the Shūichi I knew was really just a small child, and my memory had faded after so much time had passed. But then you brought me my coffee, and the moment our eyes met, all of those memories came back to me, right down to the little details. Without meaning to, I yelled, 'We meet at last!' In my whole life, I don't know if I've ever felt so happy..."

I remembered it vividly.

When our eyes met, she had definitely uttered those exact words, beaming with excitement.

"But I believed I couldn't tell you the truth then. I didn't even know if you remembered me, and I thought if you did, it would be a painful memory for you anyway. I didn't want to throw you off. More than anything though, I thought that if you knew that I'd come all the way to Tokyo to look for you because of a memory from a brief period in our childhood, you'd think the whole thing was creepy..."

"So that's why you came up with the story about our previous lives?"

I was having so much trouble connecting the pieces of her story that I blurted out the question without meaning to.

I could understand why she didn't want to tell me the truth. I definitely wouldn't have been overjoyed if she'd told me at the time why she was really there. I might even have been angry that she was digging up unhappy memories from my childhood. And I might have tried to keep her at a distance. But even still, I asked, why did she end up telling that story?

"It was really just spur of the moment. When I think about it now, it seems hopelessly stupid. But at the time, I couldn't think up any other ready explanation. I'm always so incredibly inarticulate..."

She took a deep breath then, as if she'd been straining so much to tell me all this that she'd completely forgotten to breathe.

She went on, "But, like I said before, when I'm using my imagination, I have no trouble telling stories. After you stopped coming around, I actually invented a story that you and I really had known each other in a previous life, and so we would meet again someday because we were connected by fate. It's true. I'm probably out of my mind. When I come up with a story like that, I end up truly believing it. I spend all my time thinking about things like that, trying to escape my pathetic reality...

"I could see how puzzled you were by my crazy story. But if telling you the truth meant that I would never see you again, it was much better to let you think I was crazy as long as I could still see you. But you were kind to me despite all that. You even cared so much about me that you asked me out. I know I was being selfish, but it just got more and more impossible to justify, and more and more painful to keep it up . . . I decided that I couldn't keep deceiving you and pretending any longer. I had to end it..."

As she talked her voice got weaker and weaker, almost vanishing in a faint whisper, and then disappearing for good.

The two of us said nothing for a long time. I knew, at least, that she wasn't lying. That came through clearly in her stumbling but earnest speech.

But what was I supposed to feel after hearing all of that? Was I angry at Chinatsu? No, absolutely not. But I also declined to say anything to comfort her. Sitting beside her, I couldn't look at her straight on, so I kept my eyes fixed on the empty swing, which was gently swaying in the breeze.

"That's what I wanted to tell you."

She was the one to open her mouth first. She drew a deep breath into her chest, abruptly stood up from the bench, and turned to me and bowed deeply.

"I'm sorry I took so much of your time and made you listen to this unpleasant story. I understand if you can't forgive me. So, will you please forget everything I told you? And forget about me too."

"But . . ." I knew I should say something, but she cut me off.

"Thank you for everything you've done for me. It might be presumptuous of me, but I pray, with all my heart, that you'll always be happy and healthy."

The minute she said those words, she took off without waiting for a reply. She ran for dear life, heading straight for the exit to the park. In an instant, she disappeared into the night. Left alone in the dark playground, I could only stand there dumbfounded.

"What was all that..." I mumbled, half in anger, after I could no longer see her. It was all I could do.

"What? Why?"

On Sunday, the following week, after I informed Shizuku that Chinatsu Yukimura would not be coming back to the café, she stared at me bewildered.

"Why won't she come back? Did you say something to her?"

"No."

"You're sure?"

"I'm sure."

"Then why?" Shizuku asked as she peered at my face, looking quite serious. "That's crazy. I've been looking forward to seeing her so much..."

"She's the one who made her decision. I'm not lying."

It pained me to tell Shizuku, but I had to let her know. Sure enough, I watched as Shizuku's expression clouded over before my eyes. She turned for help to her father, who was occupying his usual spot behind the counter.

"That's really it, Shūichi?" the owner asked, his voice lower than usual.

I nodded silently, not feeling up to saying anything more.

"Well, if Miss Chinatsu said so herself, then there's nothing we can do. This is a café. It's up to everyone to decide whether they come or not. It's not our decision. Shizuku, don't just stand there, help us close up."

The owner's voice sounded stern, but also somehow a little sad. After he snapped at her, Shizuku didn't seem able to say anything more. She kept her mouth shut as she went back to straightening up the chairs at each table.

On each Sunday that followed, Chinatsu failed to appear. There were no new ballerinas to add to Shizuku's tin of cookies. There were still fewer than ten inside.

The month of March went by like a dream.

The cherry trees bloomed in Yanaka Cemetery, creating a beautiful tunnel of pale pink flowers. The market street was bustling for days with the influx of people coming back from parties under the cherry blossoms. As I walked through the neighborhood, it seemed like years had passed since Chinatsu and I were strolling together down this street in the cold wind.

Still, when Sunday came around again, Shizuku was the only one who still hoped that Chinatsu might show up. She even called her cell phone several times. But her calls always went straight to voicemail.

When I looked at her, I thought to myself, What's wrong with this girl? Why should she feel so close to a total stranger who just happened to come a few times to the place her dad ran? I wanted to forget Chinatsu as quickly as I could, but seeing the disappointment on Shizuku's face every week meant there was no way I could forget her, no matter how much time had passed. What was I supposed to do? I truly had no idea.

"She didn't come again today."

After the café closed, Shizuku sat staring out the window at the spring rain. It had gone on like this for three weeks. I normally made no attempt to respond, but this time I finally gave in and asked her a question.

"Shizuku, you were saying the other day that Chinatsu

reminded you of someone. Who was that? Was it someone I know?"

A slight smile appeared on her lips, and she shook her head no, which made her long ponytail swish from side to side. "It's no one you know. It's someone who died a long time ago. So I don't get to be with her anymore. And she's someone who was really precious to me. But that doesn't matter now. It was just when I first met her. Now I like Chinatsu for who she is, apart from all that. It's strange, isn't it? A little while ago, I didn't know Chinatsu at all, and yet now a Sunday without her makes me feel so sad."

So that's how it was. Shizuku had been superimposing Chinatsu onto someone she was close to. I had no idea.

"Do you think she's all right?" Shizuku was leaning against the windowsill, staring quietly at the rain. "What does she do with her Sundays? I hope she isn't all by herself. It might not be any of my business, but I don't want her to be all alone. I'd hate for that to happen to someone I care about."

Hearing her saying this I felt a sharp pain in my chest.

I couldn't take this from a girl who was younger than me. I couldn't let the café's poster girl make me feel this way. More than anything though, I couldn't accept that things might end like this.

What was Chinatsu doing right now? Spending Sunday all alone? Each time I'd seen her at the café, every expression on her face—her shy smile, the way she fiddled with her bangs, the way she looked when she ran into the café, out of breath as the snow was falling outside—it all came back to me so vividly and then vanished.

"I understand. No one wants someone they care about to be lonely."

I patted her on the head.

And, of course, she quickly shoved my hand away.

When I arrived at the factory, it was after six. I'd deliberately aimed for that time, because I'd heard that was when she finished work. A single cherry tree stood in front of the sprawling factory lot. Nearly all of the blossoms had already dropped. The petals swirled in the breeze, drawing little circles around my feet.

I'd come all this way on a reckless whim, now I stood outside the oppressive, closed iron gate, wondering what I should do next. But after a while, a group of women who seemed like employees came out of the building, walking in a line. They remained in formation as they walked to another building along a brilliantly lit outdoor corridor.

She was with them. Dressed in dark gray work clothes and a hat, she was walking hunched over behind the other workers, who were boisterously chatting away.

She seemed so small. So terribly small.

If I called out to her from here, I thought, I might draw attention to her and make her uncomfortable. But even as I stepped out from under the streetlight, I couldn't take my eyes off her. I stood, frozen in place, staring at her in profile. Then, suddenly, she turned in my direction, and her eyes looked straight into mine.

Oh no. But I knew it was already too late. Even from that distance, I could see her go to pieces, and she came rushing over to me, half running.

"Hello," I said, trying my best to sound upbeat on the other side of the iron gate. But she was clearly upset.

"What . . . what are you doing?"

"I'm sorry to bother you here."

"No, it's okay, but why are you here?"

"Don't you remember how you ran off in the middle of our conversation? I want to talk to you."

"Oh, um, I said everything I had to say."

"That might be true for you, but I have something to say to you too. Will you go out with me?" I asked, and though she looked as if she might burst into tears, she nodded yes.

Since she still had to work overtime, she pointed me in the direction of the nearest family restaurant and asked me to meet her there. She arrived after eight thirty, two hours later, having changed from her dark gray work clothes to a more feminine white blouse and long pale blue skirt. This look suits her better, I thought to myself.

"I'm sorry I kept you waiting."

"Chinatsu, have you already had dinner?" I asked as she sat across from me, with her eyes cast down.

"Oh, um, yes, I ate something light during my break."

"Then do you mind if we go somewhere else?"

"No, um . . . where?"

"The Torunka Café." When I said this, she looked even more distressed.

"But I already said I . . ."

"Shall we go, then? I'll get you coffee."

I got her to stand up, almost by force, and we left the restaurant.

The closed sign was already hanging on the door when I opened it up and called out, "Hello."

The owner, who was inside smoking a cigarette, gave out a little shriek.

His routine was to have a smoke after the café was closed and Shizuku had gone up to their home on the second floor. She didn't look very kindly on his smoking habit because she worried about his health.

Which is to say that whenever she caught him with a cigarette, she was livid.

"Would you mind lending me the place for a bit?" I asked.

The owner looked surprised to see Chinatsu behind me, but he seemed sympathetic. "Just don't forget to lock up," he warned me. "And let's keep the smoking between us," he said and headed upstairs after concealing the evidence by shoving his cigarette butt deep into the trash.

Inside the room, the temperature was just right, neither hot nor cold. After I led Chinatsu to a seat at the table in the middle of the room, I prepared coffee for the two of us in the kitchen. In the quiet—our usual soundtrack of Chopin had already been turned off—the sound of the electric coffee grinder seemed louder than usual.

After a few minutes, I poured our coffee and took a sip to test it. The warm liquid left a faintly bitter taste before it slid down my throat. Not bad, if I do say so myself.

After I brought the coffee and sat down across from her, she spoke up, unable to wait any longer. "Um . . ."

"Yes."

"Are you angry at me?"

"I am angry," I said firmly. "It's because I'm angry that I came to see you."

When she heard that, she squeezed her eyes shut and lowered her head, as if she were preparing to be punished.

"Don't get the wrong idea. I'm not angry about what you confided in me. It took me time to process it, but I wasn't angry."

Chinatsu opened her eyes, and by the look on her face, I could tell she didn't understand at all. I urged her to drink her coffee before it got cold.

"What made me mad was that, from the beginning, you never felt that I could forgive you, or understand the reasons why you did what you did. Before you started to speak, you'd already closed yourself off. You'd made up your mind, and then you ran away. That's what angered me."

"I, um . . ." She was trying to respond, but I went on, although I felt guilty for doing so.

"But then I thought about why I was so angry. Much later on, I realized that it was because I was just like you."

"Like me?" She had just brought the cup of coffee she had been holding politely in both hands to her lips, but she stopped to ask me this, looking unsure about where the conversation was headed.

"The truth is six months ago I got dumped by the girl I was going out with. I really loved her, and I meant to take care of her, but when she broke up with me she told me, 'Shūichi, you never opened your heart to me. You were always holding back, always doubting. You were closed in on yourself.' It shocked me to hear that. I hadn't realized it, but I guess that's what I was doing unconsciously. Maybe there was a part of me that didn't fully understand what it meant to be in love."

It's true. I thought I was taking care of Megumi, but that was only for me, she never felt it. And right up until the end, I didn't notice I was destroying the very thing I treasured. That truth came as a very, very big shock.

"That day, you made the decision right from the start to declare that it would be the last time we'd see each other. When you wouldn't let me say anything in response, it made me extremely sad. I felt sad and empty. Much later on, it occurred to me that I had done the same thing to my girlfriend. I was finally able to understand what she meant. What I mean is that, that day in the park, I was overcome by anger because you showed me what I'd been like before."

After saying all this in a single breath, I took a sip of my coffee. I'd poured it a moment ago, but it was already mostly lukewarm.

How long had it been since I'd shared what I was feeling in such an unguarded way?

It might actually have been the first time in my life. I knew that it didn't have much to do with the person right in front of me, and it might even end up confusing her. But I wanted to tell her what I'd been feeling since that night. I wanted to understand how she felt too. It was a simple thing, but I hadn't been capable of it before now.

"To be honest, it made me happy to hear that you went looking for me, that you came all the way to Tokyo and spent a year of your life to see me again. It warmed my heart to think there was someone out there who cherished their memories of me."

"You didn't think it was creepy? I was sure that was how you'd see it..."

Chinatsu's voice trembled as if she couldn't possibly believe me.

"I was surprised, of course. I mean, incredibly surprised and confused, but I didn't think it was creepy. The story you told me about our previous lives was much creepier."

I'd meant it as a joke, but she looked crestfallen. "I'm truly sorry for that. I really have to apologize."

I got flustered and hurried to reassure her. "No, it's okay, please. You don't need to apologize."

"But..."

"It's okay. I understand now why you felt that it was what you should say." I smiled for her. "I'm the one who should apologize. I need to apologize to you and to your mother."

"What?"

I sat up straight, pushed aside my cup of coffee with its last remaining drops of black liquid, and faced her squarely. "I'm sorry for the terrible things my father did."

I needed to apologize as a matter of principle for what he'd done. With every ounce of my being, I bowed so low that my nose nearly touched the table.

"There's no need to... My mother and I didn't blame your father."

"But I still feel guilty for what he did."

"Maybe we should thank him instead. I mean, it's because of him that I was able to get to know you. Please lift your head," she said, on the verge of tears. "The truth is," she went on hesitantly, "I couldn't decide if I should tell you this, so I didn't mention it earlier, but your father came many times to visit my mother when she was in the hospital."

"Is that true?" What she said had an immediate impact. Without thinking, I stopped bowing and lifted my head.

"I told you that I went to your father's business to talk to him. But the fact is that he saw through me right away. He said I looked just like my mother. Then he asked me how she was doing... My mother cried a little when she saw your father near the end of her life. What's more, when your father learned that we were so poor, he helped pay the costs of her treatment and hospitalization. 'I'm sorry but this is all I have at the moment,' he said, and handed me the money.

"I tried to refuse, but he said, 'Please accept it. I'll scrape together more and bring it to you.'

"In the end, I gratefully accepted his offer and took the money."

"Is that right..."

What she said came as another profound shock. She seemed to misinterpret the worried expression on my face, and she hunched her shoulders. "It's probably because of that that your father couldn't pay your tuition. But once I get the full amount together, I'm going to pay your father back."

"No, that's not what I meant. I mean, even if that were the reason, I would be fine with it. So there's no need to pay him back. I think you telling me this has helped me a little bit. I see now that he still has a heart, and if he helped your mother even a little bit, that helps me feel better. To be honest, up until the moment you told me this, I'd planned to cut ties with him altogether."

She seemed to hesitate again, then she said something I never would have expected. "He said the way he'd treated you was unforgivable. But even though he wanted to apologize, he felt too ashamed to face you." It was so unexpected that it made me take a step back and reflect.

My resentment didn't completely disappear, of course, but I felt a weight lift off my chest.

"Okay, next time, let's go give him a punch in the face, shall we?"

"What? I mean, um, violence would be—"

"I'm joking," I said with a laugh, seeing her as flustered as expected. "But I think we'd be within our rights."

"Still, hitting someone..."

"I won't. I hate violence too. I'll try to have a good talk with him sometime. There's no point in trying to run away from him forever."

I was only able to see that thanks to the woman right in front of me. She was the one who taught me that I couldn't go on avoiding the things I didn't want to face. Of course, if I told her that, she'd probably stare back at me, dumbfounded.

The night grew late. The hands of the pendulum clock on the wall showed it was past ten. I couldn't keep Chinatsu much longer because she had to be up early in the morning.

"Sorry. I let the conversation veer off in a weird direction. I know you'd better get going soon. I might be wrong about this, but, before you leave, there's one more thing I need to ask you."

"Uh, what . . . what is it?" She sat up straight, nervous again about what I was about to say.

I still couldn't remember much from those days, but one word had popped into my head. I wanted to check if it was right.

"Is it possible that I used to call you 'Chi-chan'?"

The moment I uttered that nickname, she startled. Then her eyes grew wide for a moment before she covered her face in her hands. It happened so suddenly that I rushed to ask if I'd said something wrong, but after a pause she said, "That's right . . ." Her voice seemed to squeeze out through the gap between her fingers.

Before long, her shoulders started to tremble, and she was sobbing. She cried quietly but intensely, as if everything she'd been holding back had broken through. With the music off, the café had been terribly quiet. Now the sound of her crying echoed inside.

"I used to call you 'Shū-chan.'"

For some reason, the moment I heard her trembling voice say that name, I felt something warm welling up inside my chest.

There were tears in my eyes. I held them at bay somehow while I stood beside her rubbing her back as she went on crying and moaning.

"Is that right? Well, even if it wasn't in a previous life, the two of us really have met before. I can really feel that now. It ought to have been a precious memory. I'm sorry that I forgot."

She shook her head vigorously from side to side, still covering her face.

"Um, Chinatsu. There's something else I wanted to say. Will you hear me out?"

A large crying eye appeared in the space between her fingers, still shedding tears.

"I love you. I love you so much. So please don't just decide we won't see each other again. I hate the thought of it. I couldn't take it. If you hate me and you never want to see my face, then I'll resign myself to it. But if not, please don't decide this is the last time. Don't decide something so sad on your own. I still want to see you. Just like before, no, even more. I want to be at your side. Is that wrong?"

"It's not wrong. But why would you?" she asked, and then covered her face again and sobbed.

"Okay, will you come back to the café? Shizuku and the owner have been waiting for you."

"Are you sure it's okay? It's all right if I come to see you again, and they won't mind if I come to see them too?"

"We're the ones asking you to come," I said, sure that I could feel the warmth of her back in my hand.

"That makes me happy. Even though I'm such a lost cause . . ."

"That's not true. Don't say that."

"But . . ."

"You're not a lost cause. I know you. I can't say I know everything about you, but I know that much. You're not a lost cause. And I refuse to believe anyone who says you are," I said firmly. I'd known that for a long time. I'd learned it with each passing Sunday, the days piling up little by little like so much fallen snow.

Chinatsu still didn't know that Shizuku had been carefully storing her folded ballerinas in a cookie tin. Those ballerinas were Chinatsu herself. I saw that now for the first time. Delicate and kind, but there was something sad about them being left alone, in harm's way.

So I wasn't going to leave her alone.

To do that, I was going to have to become a little stronger. So that I could help ease the pain and sadness she'd carried all alone until now. So that I could become someone she could lean on, even if only a little. For that to happen, I needed to get better at understanding other people's pain. And one day the arch of ballerinas would be complete.

It's a wonderful thing to want to change like that for someone else.

"Hey, I think this is the right time to say it together," I said cheerfully, peering at her face, but she was still crying.

Then Chinatsu, Chi-chan, lifted her head slightly.

"Huh?"

"Remember 'Let's keep going with zero accidents'?"

At those words, the woman who now meant so much to me finally gave a little smile.

Our coffee had long since gone cold, so I hurried to the kitchen to make another cup.

Part Two

The Place Where We Meet Again

It was my first time at the café in over thirty years—though, technically, it was no longer the same place. In the days when I came here often, the café was called Nomura Coffee, and the owner was an old woman with a stoop, who must have been well into her eighties.

At the height of summer, the dust-covered air conditioner would whine as it strained to keep running, yet even just sitting there your back would grow damp with sweat. In the winter, the fire in the oil stove in the corner would glow bright red, but every draft that blew mercilessly through the interior made you wince.

Now the café at the end of that lane of homes has an odd-sounding name, the Torunka Café. The music playing from the speakers is no longer the Hall and Oates songs that you used to hear a lot on the radio in those days, but Chopin's piano compositions. The old woman is gone too, naturally. The owner is now a stern-looking man in his late forties.

It's a sad thing to realize, but the truth is I can't say I'm overly disappointed.

The days that have passed can never be recovered. I should be surprised that there was even a café here at all. Back then, there were so few customers at Nomura Coffee that one could've easily imagined the old woman hanging up her apron and closing up shop. In fact, the main reason I liked going there was that it was always empty, and you could stay as long as you liked without worrying that anyone might complain.

Still...

Before I came back, I held on to the secret hope that this place alone would remain unchanged. That if I came, it would be as if nothing had happened, and the past would begin again. That I would slip through the front door, and the old woman with a stoop would say, "Oh, welcome!" and the interior would be the same as it was before, uncrowded, dark, and vaguely gloomy, humid in the summers and bone-chilling in the winters, and I would go right back to my old four-seat table in the back, as if I had been pulled inside.

I had hoped that this place alone would have remained unaltered, as if a spell had been cast over it to stop time until I appeared again.

And, of course, I hoped that Sanae would be here. Looking as young as she did then. And that I could cast off the loose flesh from this heavy frame and become the person I once was. Young, reckless, still unfamiliar with the fear of losing it all.

Sheesh.

I sat at the counter of the Torunka, shaking my head, trying to rid my mind of these childish fantasies. The coffee left in the white porcelain cup in front of me had gone completely cold. Peering into the black liquid, I saw a dim silhouette of my face reflected back. I drank the rest in a single gulp to avoid the view.

"Can I make you another cup?" a voice called out from the

kitchen unexpectedly. It was the proprietor. I'd been coming here every day for a while, but this was the first time he'd spoken to me.

"It's on the house, in gratitude for your patronage."

I looked up to see the proprietor standing on the other side of the counter. He looked back at me as a pleasant smile appeared on his stern face. He seemed surprisingly childlike when he smiled. He always dressed in a freshly laundered and starched dress shirt with a black apron, which gave him an air of elegance and cleanliness, with his slim but muscular frame and dark complexion.

I wondered what the proprietor truly thought when he looked at the weary man, well past fifty, sitting before him, who spent every weekday afternoon lingering over his cup of coffee. No, let it go. If I start worrying about things like that, what will become of me?

"I'll take you up on that, I guess."

"Okay. Another blend?"

"Yeah." I nodded, and the proprietor's face suddenly reverted to its previous earnest expression as he set about preparing another cup of coffee.

It was a small place. With its location around the corner from the market street, down an alley surrounded on both sides by private homes, it was awfully hard to find. Based on the days I'd been coming here, I think the clientele was mostly older men and women who lived nearby. But from the proprietor's movements and the intensity of his gaze I could see clearly that he took pride in his work. He had the look of a man who approaches his work with conscientiousness and sincerity. I vaguely envied him.

"Hey," I said, following him with my eyes. It was honestly the first time I'd spoken up of my own volition in a long while.

"What can I do for you?"

"When did you take over this café?"

With the silver pour-over kettle gleaming in his hand, he never looked my way as he poured the boiling water over the coffee grounds in the filter, tracing circles in the steam. Before long, the coffee beans bloomed luxuriously as if responding to his thoughts.

"Hmmm. It's been more than twenty years."

"Twenty?"

"Yeah, the place was originally a different café. It was run by a couple, but after the husband passed away, the wife kept it going by herself. But the wife was getting to be of an age where it seemed time to close up. I'd known the couple for some time, and when I heard that, I asked to buy it from her."

"And the old woman?"

"After she gave up the café and retired, she lived in a home nearby, but I guess probably about twelve years ago she passed away."

"Is that right..."

I let out a small sigh. Still, that too was a normal consequence of the passing of time.

"Were you an acquaintance of Mrs. Nomura's?"

"I'm not sure I'd go that far. I used to come to the café often, a long time ago."

Thinking back, I can't say I ever had a private conversation with her. It was just: "Oh, welcome!" "Here's your house blend." "Thank you for coming." That's about all she ever said to me, and I simply nodded and said nothing.

"Oh, so you were a regular customer there." The proprietor's reaction surprised me. "Although we changed the exterior, we actually kept the interior basically the way Mrs. Nomura left it. I really loved the café's atmosphere."

"So that's why it still feels the same."

I looked around the inside of the café once more: the glossy amber-toned wooden chairs arranged around the tables, the dark brick wall, the plain pendant lamps hanging from the ceiling, the old pink pay phone set up outside the bathroom. They were all from that era, though like me, they looked worn down after all these years.

However, the atmosphere today was drastically different in one respect: it was much brighter now, whereas the old place was distinctively dim. Nomura Coffee felt like a cove where everything had drifted in on the wind one day and remained, settling quietly in place. The Torunka, on the other hand, felt like a place fresh air blew through. That's the impression it gave me.

"Oh, I'm happy you're here. It's amazing to get a visit from one of Nomura Coffee's regulars. Did you happen to live around here?"

I shook my head slightly. "I knew someone who did. I lived in a neighborhood two stations away."

"Ah, I see."

If you follow the Yanaka Ginza market street and then go down Yomise Street, you come out onto a big hill called Sansakizaka. Sanae lived in a two-story apartment building, right behind the little public bath in the middle of the hill.

Several days earlier, I had stopped by to check it out. The public bath was surprisingly still in business, and the neighborhood still had the same atmosphere, but her apartment building was not there anymore. In its place was a three-floor building with a narrow parking lot. But that was just another consequence of the passing of time.

Just as I was determined to get sentimental again, the proprietor placed a fresh cup of coffee before me. "Here's your house blend," he said. I watched the steam faintly rising from the cup for a moment, then I slowly reached out my hand.

"It's delicious," I said, unable to keep the thought to myself.

The proprietor gave a slight nod.

This man certainly made a good cup of coffee. The aftertaste was light and refreshing. There was no gritty, unpleasant flavor whatsoever left on the tongue. It's probably because he gave it just the right amount of time for extraction so that the flavor of the beans came through so perfectly. With each sip, I could feel it permeating my body.

Even if you put aside whatever my personal tastes are, you're not going to find coffee this good at any old café you stop into. From the taste alone, I can declare that Torunka far surpassed Nomura Coffee. And charging five hundred yen for it in today's world seems like a pretty honest price.

The moment I placed the cup back on the saucer, I heard the clear clang of the bell on the door. The bright light from the street outside shone into the café, and a cheerful voice called out, "Hello, sir!"

I turned and glanced in that direction, and saw a tall, slender woman in her mid-twenties walk jauntily into the café, dressed in what seemed to be her usual, casual way, in a gray hooded sweatshirt and jeans.

A face appeared through a gap in the short curtain hanging at the entrance to the kitchen. "Oh, Ayako, welcome back!"

"Hey, Shizuku!"

I quickly turned back.

I definitely wasn't going to say anything. I only looked in her direction when she first walked in. I focused my gaze on my cup of coffee. The door shut, and I could feel her passing behind my back, and then she and the girl had a friendly conversation.

"It's warm today. Maybe I'll have an iced tea? Hey, Shizuku, don't you have school now? It's only two o'clock."

"What do you mean? It's Saturday."

"Really? Damn, I lost track of the days because of work."

"Oh, to be such a free spirit."

"What are you talking about? I might not look it, but you'd be surprised how busy I am. It's like they say, 'One seldom finds pure happiness without a touch of sadness.'"

"Is that another one of your weird quotations?"

"What do you mean, weird? It's a quote from a famous poet. You owe Heinrich Heine an apology. But seriously, Shizuku, when is your chest going to fill out? I swear you haven't changed since grade school."

"Hey, I don't need to hear that from you. It's sexual harassment!"

"Oh, hey, excuse me," she said, her voice growing more high-pitched. Then she laughed happily. A cheerful, resonant laugh.

Her voice echoed in my ears.

What the hell did I want to do? I'd been waiting for her to arrive, but now what? I should speak to her, but I didn't know what to say. Besides, she wasn't Sanae. What was the point in clinging to her?

As if trying to convince myself, I drank down the rest of the coffee in my cup, stood up, abruptly paid the bill, and fled into the bright light of day like I was a man on the run.

The past thirty years of my life had been a series of mistakes. Each mistake built upon the last, one after the other, until the path behind me was paved with errors.

By the time I realized it, I was sliding down the slope, falling further and further, until I had nothing left.

I made my first mistake when I was twenty-one.

It was the biggest mistake of my life. I'm talking about the moment I abandoned Sanae.

Sanae was the girl I went out with when I was in college. She worked at the dry cleaner near my boardinghouse. Of course, I was just a broke student then, so a trip to the dry cleaner seemed about as far from my everyday life as going to the dark side of the moon. But in the fall of my first year of college, my aunt in Tokyo passed away, which meant I needed to go to the funeral. So I reluctantly brought my only suit. And that's when I met Sanae.

Our first encounter was far from dramatic. The first time I saw her, she had her shoulder-length hair pulled back tightly in a bun and wore no makeup, and she seemed plain and unsophisticated. There wasn't a big age gap between us, but she was totally different from the fashionable girls at the college I went to.

And yet there was still something about her that fascinated me. Like when you're walking at night with your head down, and you happen to look up at the sky and see the pale white moon shining brightly above you, and it stops you in your tracks. What I felt was that flutter of anticipation.

So I went back to the dry cleaner later on, chasing that strange sensation. I had absolutely no need to get anything dry-cleaned, but I took a faded sweatshirt and maybe a jacket with a frayed sleeve and stuffed them into a paper bag.

By the time I realized it, I was genuinely in love with her. My six-month-long effort to get close to her paid off, and once our relationship began, I hardly ever returned to my boardinghouse. I spent all my time at her apartment in this neighborhood.

With no relatives to depend on and only her job at the dry cleaner to make ends meet, she lived a very frugal existence. Her apartment with its harsh western exposure was only six tatami mats wide, a little more than a hundred square feet. Even then, it was a rather sad place for a young woman to live. The residents were a rough bunch, and we sometimes heard them arguing through the thin walls.

And yet, I took a liking to that apartment. In a way, Sanae and the apartment resembled each other. When I was in that little apartment that smelled strongly of the straw tatami and I watched her happily knitting or cooking or ironing, I felt a strange happiness welling up in my chest.

"Hiro."

She would call my name, her voice sounding a little nasal, but the tone was always warm and inviting. And every time she called my name, my heart stirred.

Hiro, what would you like to eat?

Hiro, you're quiet today, aren't you?

Hiro, did you really go to class?

Hiro, let's be together forever. From now on, let's be together forever and ever.

I felt embarrassed to respond to her openheartedly, and I tended to give only curt replies.

It was also around then that I grew attached to the area where she lived—the streets lined with wooden houses, dotted here and there with temples and shrines, the busy market street with all the different shops along the way, and the little lanes that twisted and turned until you couldn't be sure where they'd lead you. The neighborhood had a charm that you'd never find in one of those tidy residential zones organized by planning boards. I would take

Sanae on meandering walks through the area. We were exploring with the excitement you feel when you're that young, wondering what will be around the next corner, and where it will all lead.

It was during one of those freewheeling investigations of the neighborhood's backstreets that we stumbled onto Nomura Coffee. It was soon a favorite, and eventually it became where I spent most of my time, aside from Sanae's apartment.

A cup of the house blend coffee cost 230 yen. It wasn't by any means a great cup of coffee, but in those days it seemed the height of luxury.

And yet I was also hopelessly ambitious in those days. I'd fled to Tokyo as soon as I'd passed my college entrance exams, having despised the town where I was born with its industrial zone surrounded by smokestacks and the din of factories. Even after I moved, I was still smoldering inside. I was secretly dreaming that one day I would be a great success. And that I wouldn't end up like the others in my gloomy hometown, where even on cloudless days, the sun's rays barely reached us.

It was probably about a year and a half after I started going out with Sanae that a little opportunity fell into my lap. I was participating in a clinical trial lasting four days and three nights, when the guy in the bed next to me suggested we go into business together. He said his father worked in international trade, so he could take advantage of his connections to start our own import business. Did I want to join him? There was something a little hard to believe about the proposal, but I jumped at the offer. It was a chance to get ahead, and, more than anything, it sounded fun.

Despite the fact that I didn't know the first thing about European antiques, the business went almost unnervingly well. At the end of the 1970s, as Japan rapidly became wealthier, there were relatively rich people all over the country looking to buy old European furniture and tableware, but very few dealers were actually selling them cheaply at wholesale. Of course, there were no cell phones in those days, and no internet. In some cases, these people would pay ten times what it cost us for a clock or a writing desk we'd bought cheaply abroad. I was just a student, dressed in my one good suit, but they trusted me without hesitation—never noticing that under that suit, I was covered in cold sweat.

All of a sudden, I was busy. Inside my mind, the cogs were no longer stuck; they had started spinning wildly. All the spare time I hadn't known what to do with, the hours I'd spent smoldering in the café, were swallowed up by work as if by magic. I started flying overseas, hopping from country to country.

I spent more and more time away from Sanae's apartment.

A week, sometimes more than ten days at a time. And yet, when I showed up unexpectedly, Sanae would be there waiting for me, preparing a meal. She'd greet me with a smile. "Hiro, you've been working so hard." And little by little, it started to weigh me down. Rather than feeling gratitude that she was always there waiting quietly for me to return, I felt irritated. Her apartment, and the neighborhood, suddenly seemed shabby. When I looked up from the little street and saw the light shining down from her apartment window, I wondered why I'd lingered there so long.

Then, one rainy night, I stopped coming home to Sanae. Sanae would be fine, I told myself. She'll find someone better. She'll be better off with a guy less consumed by ambition. What she needs is a normal, happy life. I told myself the excuses I needed to hear, so I could move on without having to face how guilty I was feeling.

When we broke up, the tears on Sanae's cheeks glistened in the incandescent light. Feeling a need to apologize, I tried to give her some money, but she absolutely refused to accept it. In the end, she told me flat out, "The best gift you ever gave me was the coffee at that café. It was the two of us having coffee together."

She stared at me with such conviction that I became terrified that I was wrong, that I was on the verge of making a terrible mistake. But I ignored the feelings welling up inside me and rushed out into the rainy street outside, leaving her behind.

I decided I would never come back again.

Work was going well. The business expanded, and we shifted from dealing with the slightly rich to working with major clients. I was given a proper executive position and found happiness only in work.

The question of marriage came up as I approached my mid-thirties. I'd gone out with my share of women, but I had never considered getting married. Then I heard that the daughter of a very wealthy investor in our company, a woman who had met me several times at parties, had taken a liking to me.

There were major reasons for concern—she was close to twelve years older than me, had been divorced twice, and her gaudy clothing could never be mistaken for good taste, but I didn't pay much attention to that. I was attracted to what she had, and looked past her to all of those things.

That was my second big mistake.

Our proper married life together lasted less than three years. It fell apart all too soon. After a couple of years, she became infatuated with another guy, and I lost what little love I ever had for her.

But she was concerned about keeping up appearances, and

threatened that I would have to quit my job if I ever divorced her. She wouldn't let me sully her reputation. Her threats, in other words, were also her father's.

If I divorced her, I'd lose everything I'd worked so desperately to build. Anxious not to anger her, I forced myself to continue our marriage to keep up appearances. I was no longer able to put my heart into my work the way I had in the past. I lived like that for six years.

Little by little, I turned to alcohol to help me escape the pressures of my job and my life with her.

That was my third mistake.

When I was drunk, I could forget a lot of things. My worthless relationships, my lack of a future, the sense of futility that often took hold of me.

But once you sober up, the world you were trying not to face comes after you again. Bit by bit, I increased my alcohol intake until finally I began drinking at work too. Even when I ate, I ended up throwing up most of it. And yet I still couldn't quit.

Then one day, I finally collapsed and had to be taken to the hospital. I lost my job and got thrown out of the house.

And yet even then I couldn't put on the brakes. I was on a runaway train. I still had plenty of money. I went on drinking night and day. I holed up in a room in my shabby apartment and drank like I was trying to drown myself. And as I drank, I cursed the world and the person I'd become.

And when I was crying in the middle of the night, I said to myself, Tomorrow I'll stop drinking and start my life over again. Tomorrow, I'll get it together. So today, I can ... Every day I repeated the same cycle. The face I saw in the mirror, with sunken eyes, belonged to a man I didn't recognize at all.

It was around that time that I started to remember Sanae.

In my drunken state, I yearned for her. The way she looked working at her job at the cleaners. The way she held a cup of coffee in her hands. The way she called my name in her sweet, appealing voice. Although decades had passed, I could still recall it all vividly.

Those were the happiest days of my life.

And I treated them like garbage. When they were no longer what I needed, I threw them in the trash without giving them another thought. I cursed the person I'd been. I was a fool. I'd lost Sanae in order to gain what? Nothing was worth that price. I could see that now.

I wanted to see Sanae.

I wanted to see her face. I wanted to hear her gentle voice.

But, how could I show myself in my current state? How could I go back to the neighborhood looking as terrible as I did?

One day, I staggered into a private investigator's office and hired them to track down Sanae. I didn't plan on going to see her yet. I simply wanted to know how she was doing. I wanted to know how she'd spent the missing years. Had she found the happiness I'd wished for her when I left?

But the private investigator told me the cruel truth.

Sanae had died two years earlier. She'd been ill. Her cancer had returned and spread all over her body. There was no way to save her.

I was shocked. The truth reverberated inside my drunken brain.

Sanae's dead?

How could such a thing happen?

In the private investigator's office, I took the report they'd presented me and ripped it into pieces in front of them. Then I flung myself at the investigator and tried to grab him by the throat. I was ranting and raving.

"Don't mess with me, you bastard. You think you can get away without really investigating because I'm an alcoholic? Look for her again!"

The men quickly held me down, and before I knew it, I'd been tossed out of the office. I went home with the shreds of my ripped-up report. Feeling as wretched as possible, I taped the report back together and looked it over. There were other facts in it that I'd been unaware of:

Such as: the fact that five years after I'd left her, Sanae had gotten married, that she'd lived not too far from that same apartment, and that she'd had a child. And that the child's name was Ayako.

Ayako. I murmured her name in a daze.

The daughter left behind after Sanae's death.

Before I realized it, I had already selfishly started to see her name as a form of salvation.

I was in the bottom of a dark hole, and her name was like a fine thread lowered down to me from the heavens above.

I was clinging to the existence of a person I had never met, someone I had never even laid eyes on, but I resolved at last to pull myself out of the mire I'd been trapped in for so long.

The day after my visit to the Torunka Café, I walked out of the business hotel where I was staying and found myself heading over to the Torunka, despite the fact that I knew full well there was no way to relive the past.

When on earth did so many tourists start coming to the market street? In the past, no one would've thought of trekking all the way downtown to see the sights. Was this just another sign of how much time had passed? I avoided the crowded street and walked down a narrow alley, where the laundry was hanging like shop curtains from the windows of the private homes on both sides. At the end of the street, I could see a brown building whose walls were a third covered in green ivy.

I knew that it was not the same café it used to be. Sanae was gone. Even if Ayako were there, what would that change?

Yet as pathetic as that was, I couldn't think of anywhere else to go. Although I'd long since quit drinking, I found myself walking on unsteady legs, almost like I was still dreaming, and when I came to, I realized they led me to this place.

"Welcome."

The proprietor greeted me solemnly. The faint light shining through the stained-glass window gave a strange bluish hue to the seats nearby. I went to my usual seat at the end of the counter.

Ayako wasn't there. I felt a little disappointed. Though if she had been there, I would've been completely incapable of sitting there calmly. Yet I still felt disappointed, a fact that I had to admit was absurd.

At that moment, she was probably at her part-time job at the florist on Yomise Street. I knew because I'd seen her there several times myself. I could picture her greeting a customer with the same warmth as today's May sunlight. She had another job that was actually her main job, I think, but I wasn't yet aware what it was.

I ordered the house blend, the way I always did. And the proprietor responded the way he always did, with a quiet yes.

Perhaps because we'd exchanged a few words the day before, I felt more friendly with him today. I wanted to try to talk to him a little more.

It might sound strange to say at my age, but I've always been extremely shy. My gruff, unfriendly way of talking was something I'd picked up by imitating the way men talked in Yakuza movies because I couldn't bear to be looked down on.

After decades talking this way, it was too late to fix it now. I didn't bear this man any ill will, but how could I communicate that to him?

"People say coffee is bad for you. What's bad about it?" I mumbled aloud to myself, intending to start a conversation. I worried I'd botched it, but he noticed I was talking to him, and turned my way.

"Oh, people have been saying that for a long time."

"Is that right?"

"Sure..."

Silence.

I cleared my throat and went on talking.

"Is it that bad for you? I mean, is it okay to drink coffee every day?"

"Do you have trouble with your stomach?"

"No, not especially."

"In that case, I don't think there's a problem with it," he replied with a smile. "It's been established now that coffee isn't carcinogenic. Coffee does stimulate the activity of our gastric juices, so it isn't recommended for people with stomach trouble or else they might aggravate their condition."

"So if you don't have stomach problems, you don't have anything to worry about?"

"Sure. I think there used to be people who lumped coffee and cigarettes together because they thought they were both bad for your health. But coffee doesn't deserve to be treated like that. Provided you choose good beans and have the right pour-over technique, there should be almost no impact on your health whatsoever. When it comes to alcohol, or meat, or coffee, we should probably all strive for moderation."

The proprietor smiled at me, as if to say, it's simple enough.

"Moderation, you say," I said, mocking myself. I let out a long sigh. A few years earlier, I was incapable of something so simple.

To come back to this neighborhood, to get a glimpse of Ayako, I had decided to quit drinking and had thrown myself into an alcoholism treatment center where I joined a wretched troupe of people like me and even worse. There, all of us who were incapable of something so simple found a fitting punishment. We hated ourselves for reaching for a drink in the first place, and we wished we could've smashed our faces in to stop ourselves if it meant we could return to our former lives.

Well, it's over now in any case. I shook my head, trying to shake off the memories of days I wished I could forget.

"Why do so many people think coffee's bad for you, then?"

"Well, I guess from the outside it doesn't look like it's good for you. There are those coffee addicts out there, fiendishly working away while they chug coffee. If you're not eating properly and just drinking coffee every day, then it's going to take its toll on your body. I imagine people seeing that sort of thing has affected its reputation."

I wasn't sure whether he liked to talk or he was just happy to talk about coffee, but once he got going, the proprietor didn't stop talking.

"And there's the fact that in the past it was known as 'the Devil's drink,' so its bad reputation is deeply rooted."

"The Devil's drink?" I asked. I reached for my coffee, my interest peaked. Steam rose faintly from the cup. In my case, there was no doubt that alcohol was the Devil's drink.

"Up until the beginning of the seventeenth century, because it originated as a drink in Muslim countries, many people outside the Islamic world considered it an unclean drink. But the pope, I believe it was Pope Clement VIII, took a sip and was enchanted by it. To remove the stigma of uncleanness, he took the rather desperate measure of baptizing coffee, and in that way it was recognized as something Christians could drink."

"He baptized coffee? That's crazy."

I laughed as I sipped my hot coffee. I was amazed to hear it was once the Devil's drink.

"It is crazy, isn't it? Nonetheless, the pope had to have his coffee. I guess you could say he was charmed by the Devil."

"So that's why it was called the Devil's drink? Now it makes sense."

I couldn't get used to the name Torunka at first, but I could see that this was a man who knew some amazing things. And his coffee was great. It wasn't a bad name after all.

"That story is"—I cleared my throat and searched for the words to say—"pretty fascinating."

The proprietor cracked a smile, as if to say "thank you." I'd meant it as praise, but I wasn't sure it had come across that way.

I left while it was still light out.

I felt a little better than usual, perhaps because I'd had a proper conversation for the first time in a while.

Beneath a sky the pale blue of a washed-out watercolor, I

walked to the end of the narrow lane, and my feet automatically took me toward Yomise Street. Once I'd passed the rice cracker store, the pharmacy, the fish market, one by one past the usual stores, a pleasantly sweet smell came my way.

It was the florist where Ayako worked.

I might have let myself get a little carried away. Normally, I would have cast a glance as I walked by, but this time my feet came to a stop right in front. Then I gazed absent-mindedly at all the brightly colored flowers. I don't know much about flower varieties, so I only recognized the tulips and pansies. Yellow, red, purple, white. All the colors shining brightly in the sun.

"Are you looking for something in particular?"

When I turned to look, Ayako was standing right next to me, wearing an apron with the store's name on it over her usual casual jeans. Her thick, long hair was gathered together in the back, and her face wore a dazzling smile.

"Ah, no, I . . ."

I'd secretly spent the past two weeks, waiting with bated breath, trying to get close to her.

This was the first time we'd spoken. I didn't want to face her, but I felt like there was an invisible hand tightening its grip around my neck, forcing me to look straight at her.

When Ayako realized that I was staring at her, she looked back at me quizzically.

"Something wrong?"

It's nothing—

Just as I was starting to say those words, my vision suddenly grew distorted. Before I knew it, I was down on one knee. My heart was suddenly pounding. I could hear it in my head. All at once it hurt to breathe.

From the time I arrived in this neighborhood, my condition had mysteriously improved so much that I'd started to forget about it. I'd avoided destroying my liver with alcohol, but I had put an enormous amount of stress on my heart. The aftereffects continued, and from time to time, I'd feel a wave wash over me.

But the timing was ridiculous.

"Um... sir, are you okay?"

I heard Ayako's distraught voice above me. Still unable to open my eyes, I tried with all my might to nod and say yes.

"You're saying 'yeah,' but you definitely do not look okay. Wait, can you stand up?"

She grabbed my arm and pulled me up by force. Then as she supported the weight of my body with her slender shoulders, she made her way across the shop and pushed me into a folding chair.

"Can I get you something to drink? Maybe water?"

"No, I'm okay... I'll be fine if I just stay like this for a bit."

The fact that it happened the instant Ayako's eyes met mine... Maybe up in heaven Sanae was punishing me for coming back to the neighborhood.

These are the sort of stupid thoughts that went through my head as I sat there breathing feebly. At any rate, I had no other choice but to endure the pain since I'd left my medication at home.

At last, the beating of my heart quietly subsided, like a receding wave. But I worried it wouldn't be long before the aftershock hit. I couldn't stay there. I struggled to stand up on my trembling legs.

"Wa... wait... wait a second there. You need to rest. You can't get up yet. Don't you know the maxim 'Caution can at times be the greatest virtue'? Don't worry, no one's going to complain if you rest awhile."

Ayako looked me over in the dim light, then said "Right?" in a voice you might use to reason with a child, and grinned.

"Yeah, but I'm really fine now."

A customer called out "Excuse me" from the front of the shop. She hesitated, looking back and forth from me to the storefront. I looked at Ayako, pretending to be calm and composed, and then I told her to go to her customer. "I'll be right back," she said. "Please stay here." But despite her plea, when she was helping the customer, I got up and left.

Aside from going to the hospital, I spent the next three days staring at the ceiling in my hotel room. Once I took the medication I'd been prescribed, the symptoms mostly eased, but I felt dead tired, like I'd swum across the ocean.

When I showed up at the hospital for the first time in a long while the doctor seemed to drone on and on about my condition. "There isn't much time to keep postponing this—you need to make a decision. You're young, and it will probably . . ."

I listened to him with a blank look on my face.

After examining me, the doctor said, "I'm giving you this warning for your own sake." From the tone of his voice, it sounded like he was dropping the subject. "But Mr. Numata, if you're not willing to help yourself, then there's only so much I can do."

Then he sighed out of pity for me and threw up his hands.

I couldn't answer him. I didn't know what I wanted to do.

After staring endlessly at the ceiling of my hotel room, I started to feel like I needed to get some fresh air.

So I left the hotel for the first time in a long while. Outside, the sun was shining, and it was warm. The sky looked clear and wide, high above my head. The cherry trees along the street had grown fresh, vividly green leaves. I gave myself over to the gentle breeze.

The mild weather had continued for so long that I could almost delude myself into thinking I was living the same day over and over again. I think I saw a foreign film about that a long time ago. A middle-aged man is marooned in time, and keeps endlessly repeating the same day. Wasn't that exactly what I was doing now? Did he ever make it out of that endless world? I couldn't remember.

After much hesitation, I found myself going down the little lane to the Torunka. I had a craving for a cup of coffee prepared by the proprietor. I planned to go in and take my usual seat at the counter. But there was already a middle-aged couple sitting there. It wouldn't feel right sitting at a table. Just as I was contemplating coming back another time, I heard a voice call out from one of the tables. "Oh, hey there!"

I didn't need to look twice at the woman excitedly coming toward me in her gingham blouse. It was Ayako.

Ayako went on talking to me in the same loud voice, unconcerned by the fact that everyone in the café was now looking our way.

"It is you after all."

"Yes . . ." I said, feeling extremely uncomfortable. There was a high probability that she'd be here. But I never imagined that she'd remember me and start talking to me.

"It's good to see you. Were you okay after what happened? You disappeared so quickly it was almost like you ran off. I've been worried about you. I never thought I'd see you here."

I was embarrassed that I'd made her worry. But based on what I'd observed in the past two weeks, there was no way she wouldn't worry about me after what happened. Part of me knew that when I showed up here. Perhaps I wanted her to notice me. It was so pathetic I couldn't bear to think about it.

"I'm sorry for all the trouble I caused." At the very least, I had to thank her, but I was mumbling like a child who had just been scolded. She laughed away my awkward apology.

"It was no trouble at all," she said. "Are you better now?"

"Yeah."

You need to make a decision. The doctor's warning replayed in the back of my mind, but I just nodded.

"Really? That's good, then."

"Ayako, you know this gentleman?"

The proprietor—whose last name I had only recently learned was Tachibana—had come up to us as we were talking by the door and was now gazing at Ayako with a look of surprise.

"Oh, um, yes, a little bit."

"Can I get the two of you a table?"

Ayako said, "Uh-huh," and after thinking for a moment, grinned at me and said, "They say, 'Life is a get-together, to which one is never invited twice.' So shall we?" When I saw her smile, I automatically agreed.

"Aren't you hot like that? Take off your coat."

Ayako took off my jacket almost by force and hung it on the hanger on the wall, as I stood in front of our table, bewildered.

I couldn't bear to look at my jacket hanging there, looking as utterly worn out as I was.

I remained grimly silent, unsure what to talk about. When I tried to drink the coffee Tachibana's daughter had brought over, my hands were trembling so much I could barely hold it.

I panicked, worried my withdrawal symptoms had come back, but that was impossible. I hadn't had a drop in over a year. My heart was beating abnormally fast. But this wasn't another attack. It was something else.

Apparently, I was nervous. That's the reason my palms were damp and my heart was beating so fast. I hadn't felt like that in ages. But sitting across from Sanae's daughter, I was hopelessly nervous.

Ayako apparently mistook my inability to speak for ill humor.

"Um, sorry if I was too pushy. You're not from around here, are you? I was born and raised here, so I just talk to everyone really informally . . ."

I shook my head brusquely. "No, it's okay."

"Hm?"

"I mean, this is fine."

"You're sure?"

"I mean I don't mind the way you talk," I said frantically, and she flashed a smile. I couldn't look directly at it.

"Okay, great. I'll stick with it, then," she replied, and then she told me a bit about herself. Her name was Ayako Honjō; she was twenty-six. I only gave her my name. And with that same smile she said, "Are you sure you don't think I'm some crazy girl? I'm not always so overly friendly with people. I mean everyone in the neighborhood is so relaxed, and you just get kind of bored with it all, you know? Oh, would you like some of this ham sandwich? I'll give it to you as a sign of our new friendship."

I was impressed by how well she talked while stuffing her face with a sandwich she'd ordered before I came.

"I'm fine. I'm not hungry."

In fact, I hadn't eaten since the morning, but I didn't think I'd be able to get anything to go down.

"You're sure? It's delicious."

When I first laid eyes on Ayako, I didn't see much of a resemblance to Sanae. She was tall while Sanae was petite, and they each gave off a very different feeling. I guess you could say Sanae was like a flower blooming inconspicuously on the side of the road. She was a very quiet and gentle woman; she had none of the vigor and radiance of the flowers Ayako arranged out in the floral shop window. But they were definitely related by blood. Up close, you could see that Ayako's nose and ears looked like her mother's. Although they had totally different ways of speaking, Ayako had the same slightly nasal tone of voice. More than anything else though, it was in the way she squinted her eyes when she smiled that I saw clear traces of Sanae, and it left me shaken.

Anyone would probably have laughed at me, if they knew everything I was feeling at that moment just because I was meeting the daughter of an old girlfriend. Even I thought it was absurd. But I was sure that the sole person I'd loved in the fifty years I'd been alive, a woman I thought I'd never see again, still existed within Ayako. The nostalgia and the love I felt then were going to break my heart.

"Hm?"

For some reason, after she had devoured her entire sandwich, Ayako stared at me with a puzzled look on her face.

"Um, this just occurred to me, but have we met before? Like maybe a long time ago?"

"No, I don't think so."

I was so taken aback by her question that I rushed to deny it. Aside from the past two weeks, we'd never seen each other before.

"Oh, okay. It somehow felt like it wasn't the first time we'd seen each other. It could just be my imagination, but I felt like we'd met before."

Ayako mumbled as she reached for the little pitcher of milk and slowly poured some into her coffee. She gently stirred the spiral of white cream drawn on the black surface of her coffee until the color turned a rich, velvety brown. It reminded me that Sanae was also the kind of person who couldn't drink coffee without adding a large serving of milk. Since I believed that the ultimate way to have pour-over coffee was to drink it black, whenever she did this, I would look at her with disapproval, and she would get annoyed and say, "It's not like you're going to drink it, so it's fine."

"Sorry if that sounded weird. I mean, 'Haven't we met somewhere before?' is an old pickup line, right? Wow, now I sound like I'm hitting on you." Ayako smacked herself on the side of her head, mocking herself. I was still at a loss for what to say, and she seemed to be worrying about what I was thinking. I took a breath and gulped down the rest of my coffee. As the warm liquid slid into my empty stomach, I felt myself become a little calmer.

"So you work at the florist shop?"

"Yeah, part time. I've known the owner and his wife since I was a kid, so they let me help out a little. I'm an illustrator, that's my real job more or less. Well, I can't make a living off it, which is kind of sad."

"Is that right?"

I didn't expect that. Sanae was particularly good at sewing and knitting, but when it came to drawing, she was terrible.

"I gave it my all as a freelancer. But there were all kinds of issues. Last month, a job I'd been working for a long time ended, and now my only freelance job is doing little illustrations for a magazine about prizes and contests."

"Really?"

"How about you?"

"How about me?" I said, repeating the question because I didn't understand it.

"I mean, how about your job?"

"Oh, um . . . up until recently, I was in the import-export business."

"Ooh, and now?"

"Now, I . . ."

"I'm asking too many questions, aren't I?"

"Not at all. I'm not doing anything at the moment. Nothing at all really."

"Oh. Well, I guess that's how it goes sometimes."

Her awkward attempt to stay positive left me feeling miserable. I took another sip of my coffee.

"You reap what you sow, you know. I have no one to blame but myself."

"But, you know what they say, 'Do not, for one repulse, forgo the purpose that you resolved to effect.'"

"Sorry, what?"

This girl sometimes blurts out some strange things.

"It's another maxim. I've loved them since I was a kid, and whenever I come across one that sounds like it might be useful, I jot it down. Even though the owner here laughs at me about them. That one was from Shakespeare. It basically means: Don't just quit if you make a mistake. You can start over again too, you know."

"Impossible."

"That was fast." Ayako laughed. Her expression could change so quickly. "Well, that's what I believe anyway. When things don't go well, you might think 'damn it,' but sooner or later what happened to you is going to become something that sustains you in the future. And when you start something new, there'll be hassles too, but it'll be exciting, won't it?"

"Well, aren't you an optimist?"

"That might be my only redeeming feature. When my mom died three years ago, I felt so empty, I was just an empty shell of myself, but then I decided I can't let myself stay this way."

"I see," I mumbled, staring at my cup of coffee. Sanae had managed to raise an amazing daughter.

"Yeah, so let's push ourselves—you know, without overdoing it. 'The world is a fine place and worth the fighting for.' That's what the great American writer Hemingway said."

As she recited the quotation, she raised her hand and flashed a peace sign.

That's how the two of us spent about an hour in conversation. Although she was the one doing most of the talking, and I merely nodded along, it really felt good. When we parted ways, I gathered what little courage I had and said, "Can we talk again sometime?"

For a moment, Ayako's eyes widened as if I'd caught her off guard, but she quickly smiled and replied, "Of course."

"Hiro . . ." I heard my name, and when I turned around, Sanae was there. Back in that modest, six-tatami room. Her apartment was all the way at the end of the second floor of a two-story apartment building. The pungent smell of tatami mats. The glare of the setting sun, coming in through the window, shining squarely on the tatami.

I was sitting by the window. The world outside had taken on the color of the sunset. Night would soon reach this neighborhood of little houses with low eaves. The telephone poles and roof tiles turned orange in the light, and the people walking in the streets were trailed by long shadows. I could hear the sound of children laughing and playing nearby, and farther away, an ambulance siren that gradually faded into the distance.

I seemed to be dreaming of those days again.

"What are you thinking about?"

In my dream, Sanae spoke to me as she sat with her back straight and her legs bent beneath her, knitting something. She was in her usual spot, sitting on her red floor cushion.

"Nothing. Just looking outside," I said, thinking to myself that all this had actually happened before.

"Hiro, you're such a romantic."

"What do you mean?"

What Sanae said struck me as strange. It surprised me.

"I mean, you always stare out the window like that at sunset."

"Only once in a while."

"Is that right?"

"It is," I insisted, but she just looked back at me, trying not to smile.

"You like the sunset in this neighborhood?"

"I don't know. The sunset's the same everywhere."

"Well, I like it." Sanae had come over and sat down quietly beside me. "When I look out from here and watch the sun go down on this little neighborhood, I feel content, and a tiny bit lonely."

"Now who's a romantic?" I said and laughed.

"I am, of course. Didn't you know?"

The last daylight shone on her smiling face and turned it the same orange hue of the neighborhood at sunset. She looked beautiful. I felt it deeply. And I was overwhelmed by the quiet realization that there were things in this world that were so beautiful, and if I just reached out my hand, they were close enough to touch.

I kept staring at her. I couldn't look away.

"What is it?" asked Sanae, who had been looking outside before she turned to me.

"Nothing at all." I looked away, too embarrassed to speak. If I had told her she was beautiful, how would she have reacted? She probably would have laughed out of surprise, and said, "Next you're going to tell me it's going to snow in May." I found it hopelessly frustrating to express my feelings. But I wanted her to understand; I wanted to tell her even a small part of what I was feeling, so I did my best to find the words.

"I like watching the sunset from here too," I said. "I like it when the two of us sit side by side and watch the sunset together."

She smiled gently. Then, as if she was thinking it over a little, she turned to face the sky, with a sad look in her eye.

"If you and I ever go our separate ways, I'll remember us watching the sunset together from here. No matter how many years go by, no matter how many decades pass, I know I'll remember this. When will we ever see the evening sky looking this beautiful again?"

I probably stared at her with a dumb look on my face. As if trying to avoid my gaze, she said, "I'm sorry if that sounded weird. I suppose I should start making dinner soon." Then she quietly got up and walked away from the window.

That will never happen, I thought. We'll always be together from now on. We'll grow old together.

If I had been able to say those words aloud as she turned away from me, would our futures have turned out differently? That's the question I asked myself, still half asleep.

But the version of myself in the dream said nothing. I merely sat there by the window.

And I went on sitting there as I watched the orange sky give way to darkness.

"Hiro..."

I was walking down the street with my shoulders hunched, when someone suddenly called out and startled me.

"Oh, does that bother you? But it's your name, isn't it? Hiroyuki Numata? I figured I ought to call you by your name. Or would it be better if I shortened it to Numa-san?"

Ayako was standing right in the middle of the Yanaka Ginza market street, dressed in a gray sweatshirt with her long hair pulled back. I let out a little sigh, discreetly enough for her not to notice. When she called my name, for a moment I lost my bearings, and couldn't tell if I was dreaming until the moment I turned around.

"Are you going to the Torunka Café? If you are, let's go together. I got a potted plant from work today, and I was just bringing it over. I'm hoping the owner can maybe keep it by the window. Look, it's an amaryllis," Ayako said, holding up the clear plastic bag in her hand. A swollen bud had only just begun to sprout from the plant in the little pot. But I probably wouldn't have known it was an amaryllis even if it was already in full bloom.

Ayako and I started to walk together down the market street.

"Nice weather again today," she said, sounding carefree as she looked up at the clear sky.

"It is, isn't it?"

"The clouds are like cotton candy."

"They are, aren't they?"

"Tomorrow will be sunny too."

"It will, won't it?"

"Actually, no. The forecast is for clouds tomorrow. That was a trap. Hiro, you're giving pat responses today."

She gave me a little punch in my upper arm. Every time Ayako called me Hiro, I got goose bumps in the small of my back. But that's what she'd decided to call me.

"Oh, uh sorry..."

"Well, I'll let you buy me a coffee."

"Sure."

"I'm kidding. I'm kidding. I'll pay. Do you think I'm some kind of freeloader?"

"No, but you were saying you haven't had much work lately."

"I have enough for coffee. As a freelancer, I have to look ahead and save up for the future. But you're the one without a job. Are you okay not working?"

"I'm fine for now," I said. "I have enough to spare."

"Whoa." Ayako let out a funny groan. "How much did you put away? We've got to show each other our bank books next time. And whoever has less wins the whole pot. 'Give to the hungry thy bread,' you know."

"I'm going to decline that offer."

"That was fast."

We walked together, hardly paying attention to where we

were going, then turned and went down a little side street one might easily have overlooked.

I ran into Ayako two times after that at the Torunka Café. The first time we only greeted each other in passing, but the second time we had a little conversation. She did most of the talking just like before, and I was never quite sure if I was properly filling in the gaps in the conversation, but I was happy nonetheless to be there.

That's all it took to lift my spirits so much it was actually a little disconcerting. I felt like I'd found a new reason to stay in the neighborhood. Until I'd spoken with Ayako, I'd spent my time there unable to get my bearings, feeling like a stranger in a strange land. But once I'd started talking to her, the distance I felt between me and everyone in the neighborhood seemed to go away, and I felt like I was a part of things again. More than anything else, that's what made me happy.

Now what concerned me was Ayako. That time I let myself get carried away and said, "Can we talk again sometime?" What did she really think? Of course, she didn't know that I was her mother's old boyfriend, the guy who had mercilessly cast her away. No, to her I was just a gloomy middle-aged man she'd happened to meet one day. If I seemed suspicious, well, I couldn't deny it.

But I couldn't see any sign that she was unhappy or bored as she joked around, walking with me. Far from it—provided I wasn't misreading the situation—she even looked like she was having a good time. Or was she that good at hiding her true feelings? As far as I knew, she was equally as good-natured as Sanae. So it was possible that she'd decided to take pity on a middle-aged man who'd obviously seen better days.

Well, there was no point in being suspicious for no reason.

You can never know what's in someone's heart. Until I came back, I never imagined that I would be able to speak with Ayako. Now she was talking to me, and that was enough.

Coming into the Torunka, we again sat down across from each other at a table.

I ordered my usual, the house blend, and she ordered a café au lait.

Tachibana began to prepare our orders, putting the coffee beans in the grinder. The sunlight passed silently through the stained-glass windows. Ayako said, "It's so relaxing here," sounding right at home as she tossed her large shoulder bag beside her.

An old man with white hair whom I always saw at the café—I think his name might have been Takita—was sipping coffee and rambling to Tachibana.

"This neighborhood's really changed, hasn't it? In the old days, the kids would be out playing in all the empty lots. Now it's just houses. Even the stray cat population has shrunk."

Tachibana responded with a forced smile. This too was a familiar sight now.

Before long, our coffee was brought to us by a young man working part time at the café. Ayako chatted with him as she gave him the plant.

"Why, hello there, child laborer."

"I'm definitely not a laborer and I'm certainly not a child. But thank you for the flowers as always."

There was always something cool about him. He seemed remarkably unlike most young people. He had none of the glaring obstinance that's characteristic of that age. And yet he still managed to be attentive in his own casual way. I have to say I didn't dislike that about him. Ayako and he seemed fairly close.

"Hey, did you go to the one-box sale at the secondhand book fair?"

"Of course I did." They seemed to be having a great time together, talking about something people from the neighborhood would know.

"By the way, Shūichi, I heard from Shizuku that you're working another part-time job. That must be hard. Are you okay with your job search for after you graduate?"

"I'm working hard at both."

"Wow, you've really become a stand-up guy. Not that long ago you were talking about wanting to repeat the year."

"That's the old me. These days I'm a man of my word," the young man said with his usual calm. "Enjoy," he added, then gave a slight bow and withdrew into the kitchen.

"It's good to be young. It took him barely a moment to become so resolute. That's love for you," Ayako said softly as she watched him walk away. Then she came out with another strange quotation. "O, 'tis Love that makes us blissful. O, 'tis Love that makes us rich."

I was so dumbfounded I interjected, "But you're still young. Don't you have a boyfriend?"

"Me? No. Nothing like that for me lately. I've decided that for now I need to put all my energy into my work."

After she took a sip of her café au lait and licked the froth from her upper lip, I awkwardly asked if she thought love and work could coexist. "So, that's how it is?"

"That's how it is. But I know I definitely want to have a family. Once work settles down, I've got to do my best to find a husband," she said with a lighthearted laugh.

There was a part of her that was strangely farsighted, almost philosophical, and there was another part of her that was almost childish. It was all out of balance. But I think that might also have been part of her charm.

"But how about you? Do you have a family?"

"No." I shook my head. "I was married once, but it fell apart."

"Oh, is that right?" The troubled look returned to her face just like when we discussed work. Her reactions were easy to read—another thing she'd inherited from her mother. I didn't want to dwell on something so dull, so I changed the subject. "By the way," I said, "it seems like you've been coming to this place for a long time."

"I've been coming since I was in middle school. Shizuku—I've known her since before she was in kindergarten. And as you can clearly see, I've had an influence on her and the way she talks, I mean, for better or for worse. Toshiko—she's the owner's wife—is living in another country now, but she was really good to me back then."

"Oh, I see."

The café seemed to matter a great deal to Ayako. Maybe as much as Nomura Coffee had mattered to me. To satisfy my curiosity, I said, "You're always carrying out such a giant bag," gesturing with my chin to the bag she'd placed beside her. She always had that leather bag with her, even though it was far too big for just puttering around the neighborhood. I was getting curious about it.

"Oh, this? It's because I keep my sketchbook in it."

"And your drawings are in that sketchbook?"

That's what I'd guessed, I thought to myself, and leaned forward slightly. I had to see what Sanae's daughter's drawings looked like.

"Well, I mean, nobody writes a novel in one of those."

"May I see them?"

"Uh, sure, but they're just doodles."

She handed me the sketchbook, making clear that she was a little embarrassed.

Inside that thick sketchbook were drawings, I guess you could call them, in pencil, of things like the homes and stores along the streets nearby, stray cats, the view from the florist shop where she worked, and old people sitting on a bench on the side of the road. She'd even drawn the view of the interior of the Torunka from the seats we were sitting in at that very moment. The light coming in through the window, the calm, dim atmosphere, the warmth of the interior . . . the picture managed to convey all of it.

"I just sketch the things I see on my walks, partly just to practice," Ayako said casually, but I was impressed that she drew something of that quality just for practice.

With only black lines on the cream-colored pages of her sketchbook she had been able to capture the atmosphere of the neighborhood. I turned the pages, gazing in admiration. It was like you could see the neighborhood living and breathing in the pages of that sketchbook.

"Wow." I was genuinely marveling at Ayako's drawings.

"No, they're really just doodles."

"Doodles? No way. These are far beyond that. You can draw this well but you can't get a job?"

"No, no, there are tons of people who can draw better than that, people with their own unique style."

If that was true, then being an illustrator had to be a tough job. How could she have thrown herself into a world like that? As I clung to the sketchbook, I muttered my concerns to her.

Ayako laughed. "That was thanks to my mother."

Before I knew what I was doing, I looked up and asked, "Your mother?"

"Yeah. When I couldn't decide if I should go to art school, and again when I couldn't decide if I should go for a full-time job or freelance, my mother was the one who was there encouraging me. 'If it's what you want to do, then you should do it,' she told me. After my father left when I was a child, my mother worked at the dry cleaner, and we didn't have much money to spare. Yet she always said, 'Don't worry about money. Your dreams are my dreams.' Still, art school tuition is no joke, you know."

"Is that right?"

I thought to myself, That sounds like Sanae. It's just like her.

"That's how she was. She always put me ahead of herself. She supported me and raised me all on her own."

"Is that right?" I understood now. I could picture it all.

"Yes." Ayako kept her mouth closed for a while. She narrowed her eyes. "It used to weigh on me sometimes, how kind and loving she was. Even though she did so much for me, I wasn't able to thank her. But I thought if I did amazing work one day, I would surprise her. Like I could show her, 'Look, your daughter did this incredible thing.' And that would make up for not saying thank you. I never thought she'd die so soon. It's just like the line 'An opportunity is rarely recognized until it's gone.'"

"Was she sick?" As I asked the question, I felt a pain in my chest, like something constricting me.

Ayako sighed, and when she answered, her voice was much quieter than usual.

"Yeah, it wasn't long after they found the cancer. It didn't even take a year."

"Oh."

"Sorry. When I start talking about my mother, I get depressed. I can't help it. Well, anyway, the reason I'm working hard now is thanks to my mother. So, I have to live in a way that wouldn't embarrass her. That's what I meant when I told you before about wanting a family. It's because I admire my mother so much that I want to be a mother too someday," Ayako said, regaining her usual cheerfulness.

It might have been my imagination, but I thought I could still hear a trace of sadness in her voice.

"I'm sure . . ." It was the conventional thing to say, but I felt I had to say it: "I'm sure your mother is up there rooting for you."

Ayako sat there for a moment blinking, then she smiled. "You're right, you know. I really believe that."

"I believe it too," I said with conviction.

It must have come off as funny to her, because she furrowed her brow and started to laugh. "That doesn't sound like you at all," she said with a teasing grin.

"Sure it does," I said, but my irritated response only made her laugh more.

"Well, we've only just met so I'm sure there are a lot of things I don't know about you. Let's leave it at that. But, anyway, if you're interested, I could do a drawing of you," she said abruptly.

"Me?"

"Yeah, if here works for you, I could do it in less than ten minutes. Hiro, you have a distinctive face. I think it'll be interesting to draw you."

Ayako opened her sketchbook and held her pencil in her hand with a mischievous grin on her face. I rushed to turn her down. There was no way I could ask her that. It was too embarrassing. "Nah, let's drop it for now. Maybe one day."

"Oh, that's disappointing. Don't you know the line 'Write it on your heart that every day is the best day in the year'?" Ayako said, clearly sulking.

In June, the midday sun became a bit more intense.

I kept up the same routine each day, and before I knew it, I had spent over a month in the neighborhood. The amaryllis neatly displayed in the bay window of the Torunka Café had already produced a bright red flower—which was how I learned what an amaryllis flower looked like. It was an odd-looking flower, shaped like a trumpet—and it was quietly basking in the sunlight shining in the window.

"So."
"What can I get you?"
"It's hot today, isn't it?"
"It is."
"It'll be summer soon."
"After the rainy season comes."

Tachibana and I went back and forth like this. It was already becoming a normal routine at the Torunka.

After noon, when the café was relatively empty, it felt so pleasant that I sometimes stayed longer than I meant to.

"It looks like Ayako isn't going to show up today. She tends to follow her own whims, so you never know when she's going to come. And I think sometimes she's up all night working on her illustration projects," Tachibana said, perhaps assuming that I was bored.

"I don't mind. She's just an acquaintance really. Actually, could I ask you something?" I was hoping to take advantage of the fact that Ayako wasn't there, and that there weren't many customers, to ask about something I'd been wondering about.

"What is it?"

"What made you want to run this café?"

Tachibana's usual frown turned into a grimace. He folded his arms, and let out a short, low "Mmmm..."

"Sorry, it's fine if you don't want to talk about it."

I was afraid I might've gotten carried away and crossed the line. In all our chats, Tachibana had never once asked me about my life or my past. I figured I'd screwed up again.

"That's not it. It's just not that interesting. But if you still want to hear it, I'll tell you."

I was relieved to see that Tachibana didn't seem particularly bothered by my question.

"If you don't mind."

"It's a common enough story. I used to be a salaryman. Then I quit my job."

"You in a nine-to-five job? It's hard to imagine," I said, blinking in disbelief. It seemed like he was born standing behind that counter, proudly making coffee. That's how well the job seemed to fit him now.

"Well, I don't know if you could say I was a salaryman. I worked in collections for a financial company. Now, it wasn't some shady company giving out illegal loans, but the fact is, it wasn't a job I felt good about doing. It meant you were fleecing people who didn't even have enough money to pay for their next meal."

I was genuinely surprised to find out what lay behind that stern face. When I imagined him coming to collect debts with that stern face and a stern feeling lurking behind it, his sturdy shoulders squared up to intimidate, I started to sympathize with the people in debt.

"Still, it was my job, and we had quotas, so I worked hard at it. I had a family I needed to provide for. But the thing is, doing a job like that for such a long time warps your mind. When you look at the clients, all you see is money."

"I see."

I had a similar experience. When I started the job, the rich guys who were our customers were just bundles of cash to me. As time went on, I stopped doubting whether I should see them that way.

"Then one day, one of my clients, a guy in his forties, slit his wrists in the bath. Actually, he very nearly lost his life. I happened to be paying him a visit at home right at that moment, and I rushed to call an ambulance. This guy, he was a gambling addict, and he was in pretty deep to other companies too. He was backed into a corner. It was what you might call a no-win situation."

"No-win?" I repeated what Tachibana had said, and a feeling of shame came over me.

"But don't you think it's ridiculous to die just because of money? Yet I was the one pursuing him. And until that moment, when I looked at him I only saw money. When I realized that, I felt sick at heart. Fortunately, I happened to be there, but if not, he would've certainly died. The thought of it made my hair stand up and made me break into a cold sweat. I suddenly realized how terrible my job was, and it weighed on me."

After saying this, Tachibana paused for a moment as if he was remembering that period of his life. "One moment please," he said, and then after asking for permission, he began rummaging in a drawer. Then he looked around to check the situation and lit a cigarette. Wasn't this the same guy who'd insisted that we shouldn't lump coffee together with something definitely harmful like tobacco? At this moment, he was taking long drags of his cigarette and exhaling with obvious satisfaction. I thought I should say something, but I wanted to hear the rest of the story, so I decided it was best to avoid mentioning it.

"When he was out of the hospital, I dragged him over to the office of a lawyer I knew, and he gave him advice on how to consolidate his debts. I told him that now that things were a little easier, he had to give up on the idea of dying. Naturally I knew I wasn't supposed to do something like that. I mean, I was a debt collector, after all. If he was going to exercise his legal rights, we would comply, but it was absurd to expect us to be the ones to explain those rights to him.

"Of course, as soon as my superiors learned what happened, they fired me. It was right after my older daughter was born. After a lot of worrying over things, I decided I wanted to run a café in the neighborhood. It was a childhood dream of mine. So I asked Mrs. Nomura if I could buy the place that she had just closed. I used all of my savings, took out a loan, and it still wasn't enough, so we also got assistance from my wife's family. The preparations alone took half a year. Even I was shocked by how big a risk I was taking. But after that, I had a job where I could get to know my customers individually, and where what I made could put a smile on their faces."

I felt overwhelmed at that moment as I sat in the café—it was just like Ayako's drawing. There are so many kinds of people in this world, and so many things you won't know if you never stop to ask. I didn't know quite how to put it into words, but I felt it keenly.

"Whatever happened to that guy?"

"Several years ago, he came by the café and thanked me, in tears. He said, 'You're the reason I'm alive today.'"

"Wow, really?"

"No, that was a lie."

"What!?" Having completely fallen for it, I now cried out inanely. Tachibana smiled to say *I got you*.

"If that had happened, it would've made for a nice story, wouldn't it? But actually I never saw him again. He never uttered a word of thanks after all that. There were times when I felt angry at him. It was his fault I'd lost my job and my family almost ended up in the streets. But now I'm grateful to him. It was an opportunity for me to reexamine my life. If not for what happened, I wouldn't be here, hard at work making coffee every day. I'm not saying that this was the right path for me. But what happened that day gave me a chance."

Tachibana smoked his cigarette right down to the filter, and then crushed it in the ashtray. "So I hope he's doing well, and if he wants to come by someday, I hope he does," he said, ending his speech on a magnanimous note.

"Is that right? I'm sorry for prying."

"It wasn't a very interesting story, was it?"

"No, it was interesting. It was very interesting actually," I said in all sincerity.

I was savoring my coffee and lingering in the afterglow of the story he'd told me when the door opened with a loud bang, and I looked up and saw Tachibana's daughter come flying in like a hurricane. "Dad! You were smoking, weren't you!"

When Tachibana realized it was his daughter, his confident, macho demeanor seemed to vanish into thin air, and he looked back at her like a frightened rabbit.

"N-n-no, Shizuku. I wasn't."

"What do you mean, you weren't? Then what about this cigarette butt? Mr. Numata doesn't smoke. That only leaves you."

"Hey, I was just cleaning up, and I must've forgotten that, right, Numata?"

"There's no point in lying to me! You tried to sneak it because I wasn't here. It's fine if you don't want to quit. But you're the one claiming that you're quitting. You're the one saying that smoking does only harm and no good. And you're the one who declared that you'd pay me a million yen if I caught you smoking. You shouldn't say that if you can't live up to it. Now you're sneaking around like a teenage delinquent. So, go right to the bank and withdraw that million yen. That is, if you've got the money!"

I sat there dumbfounded, watching the two of them go back and forth, when suddenly, and I mean absolutely suddenly, I was overcome by the urge to laugh. What was going on in this place? What was going on with this family?

I laughed so hard I couldn't believe it myself. I laughed so hard my shoulders shook and I let my head rest on the counter. How many years had it been since I'd laughed from deep down in my belly like that?

I was rolling around laughing. Tachibana and his daughter stopped their peaceful war of words and looked at me, baffled, unable to figure out why I was laughing so hard.

The look on their faces was so funny and, for some reason, so irresistibly lovable, that it made me laugh even more.

"Hiro, something's different about you," Ayako said unexpectedly as the two of us were having coffee together in the early afternoon, as usual. She was staring at me as if she was studying my face.

"Different about me?"

"Yeah, it's almost like you're softer now than when we first met."

"I don't think my weight has changed . . ."

"That's not what I mean. Not that kind of softness," she said, waving her hand, with an exasperated look on her face. "It's like when we first met, you kind of seemed like you wanted to keep your distance from people. I just meant that now you seem maybe a little softer around the edges."

"Is that right?" I shrugged. I didn't feel any different.

"Yeah, part of you is a bit mysterious, right? And as a result, you can be hard to get close to, but that's mostly faded away, I think."

"There's nothing mysterious about me."

"Oh, you're mysterious all right. Like, I don't know what you do, or where you live. You're a man of few words. You're like James Bond. And yet you can also be surprisingly kind."

I didn't know how to respond. I had no idea she felt that way. I'm definitely not James Bond. I'm not that intimidating, and I'm not going to turn around and fire off a round at someone just for coming up behind me. But beyond all that, I don't believe I'm a kind person.

"I'm just a guy with a lot of time on my hands." I sipped my coffee after giving Ayako my concise reply. "I don't have a place right now. I live in a hotel."

"Mmmm. Even more mysterious. Well, I like you, Hiro, even with your mysterious side," Ayako said. A smile appeared on her face like a flower in full bloom, and I nearly dropped my cup of coffee.

"Huh?"

"No, no, no, I don't mean like that. I mean like you as a person. Sort of like an older friend? I like talking to you. And more than anything, when we're together, I just kind of feel at ease," Ayako said, and then she took a sip of very milky coffee and smiled.

"There's no way that's true," I replied, getting a little irritated. "I make everyone uncomfortable."

"Maybe, but I'm not everyone. And Shizuku's always saying Mr. Numata's an interesting guy."

"You don't have to treat me with kid gloves. You're probably just here because you've taken pity on me. You're trying to cheer up a lonely middle-aged guy. Because you can be nice to anyone."

As I said this, I felt more wretched than ever. Even though I believed it was true, it hurt more to say it out loud.

But Ayako suddenly raised her voice. "What? You think I'm some kind of saint? Don't you know the line 'A friend to all is a friend to none'? I'm not that arrogant, and I don't have that much free time on my hands. I'm doing this because I like talking to you, Hiro. You've lived twice as long as I have, do I really have to explain this to you?"

"But . . ." I tried to keep arguing with her, but she glared back at me.

"There is no 'but.' If you keep talking, I really will get mad at you."

"I can't have that . . ."

"Well, that's the end of the conversation, then."

And with that final word, Ayako ended the conversation.

How can I explain how I felt then?

Being with Ayako always lifted my spirits. Of course, I doubt she does it intentionally. But how much had talking to her helped me? Merely spending time with her could make even my fears about the next flare-up go away. In fact, I could even believe the doctor's diagnosis was wrong, that the bomb I felt like I'd been carrying around inside me only existed in my imagination. After spending the day with Ayako, I would go back to the hotel feeling calm, and I could fall asleep right away. Her presence was enough to protect me from my own anxiety and restlessness.

Sheesh, I'd somehow become completely dependent on a girl young enough to be my daughter.

"So, that hotel you're living in, where is it?"

The next day, Ayako asked me this as she wolfed down a plate of chicken curry. She'd shown up at the Torunka two days in a row, which was unusual for her.

"There's a business hotel all the way down Shinobazu Street. Do you know it? That's the place," I replied, unsure what she meant by the question. At any rate, this was a girl who could eat. I had no idea how all that food could fit in her skinny body. Since I was dining mainly on rolls from the convenience store, I found it hard to believe.

"Oh, yeah, that place. Isn't it pretty expensive? I was thinking, why don't you rent a place? Living in hotels costs money."

"Too much trouble."

"You on that again?"

Ayako furrowed her brow and gave me a stern look. It's what she always did when I gave her an answer she didn't like.

"I was thinking it over last night. I think it would be good for you to move into your own place in the neighborhood. It would be a lot more convenient that way. And besides, you're going to have to get a job again sometime. This is a good neighborhood too, right? Everyone is friendly, no one's rushing around, the market street is lively, and there are lots of cafés. Aside from the trouble it would take, are there any other reasons for you not to, Mr. Mysterious?"

"I told you there's nothing mysterious about me," I said sullenly.

"Well, so then it's fine, right?" Ayako replied without missing a beat. There was no trace of ill will in her face. "Maybe you think it's none of my business? I'm just saying what I was thinking about you as your friend. Considering that I'm the one who brought it up, how about I help you find a place?"

"No, that's not what I meant. I just wasn't even thinking about it."

I'd never dreamed that I could live here. I'd never even considered the possibility. I figured I'd be leaving at some point. It seemed normal. But faced with this unexpected prospect, I was feeling shaken. This was Sanae's neighborhood, and now it was the neighborhood where Ayako was living. Now I was talking about putting down roots here, finding a job, starting a new life.

"That might be okay."

"Ah, is that enthusiasm?"

Ayako's eyes gleamed with a childlike sense of adventure. "In that case, I'll introduce you to a realtor I know."

But, with my life, there was no reason I should've expected something like that would go well.

The flare-up that brought me down in front of the florist's was nothing compared to the one this time.

I was in the shower at night when it happened. Without warning, I felt a sudden pain in my chest. It was unbearable, and it knocked me flat on my back, smacking my head against the hard bathroom floor. With hot water raining down on me, I tried to get out, crawling on my hands and knees, stark naked, and headed for the bed, dripping wet. Somehow I got hold of the room phone. I have absolutely no memory of what I said into the receiver, which was a direct line to the front desk, but I managed to get a few words out. I was out of my mind.

I don't know how much time passed after that. As I drifted off, I could hear the sound of someone knocking urgently at the door. When I opened my eyes again, I was lying in a bed in the hospital.

According to the doctor, I was knocked out for more than a day. The situation was rather serious when they got me into the ambulance. My head was wrapped in a white bandage, I guess from when I hit the bathroom floor.

When I woke up, I was shaking all over. Not because of the fall, because of the way I'd acted when the flare-up struck again. I crawled to the phone beside the bed, trying to get help one way or another. To be honest, I really wasn't that afraid of dying. The doctor used to get exasperated with me and say, "You really want to die, don't you?"

And yet, in that instant, what I felt was unmistakably a fear of dying. I thought to myself, I don't want to die. Death meant that I would cease to exist in this world without ever getting to say goodbye to anyone, and that was absolutely terrifying.

"Anyway, I'm glad you're okay," the doctor said at my bedside, speaking to me in a loud and clear voice. "But I can't guarantee you'll be okay next time. Are you really content to live like this? I'm saying this out of concern for you."

I couldn't answer him.

At this point, if you don't get an operation, you have half a year left.

The doctor had delivered that sentence after I'd been taken to the hospital following my first flare-up. That was three months ago. In other words, I now had less than three months left. Just when I'd finally found a way out of the hell of alcoholism, and could see a faint glimmer of hope, this is what I get. I guess you could say I'd brought this upon myself, but it all felt so hopeless.

The chances of success with the surgery were a little under 60 percent, the attending physician told me then. "You're still young though. It's definitely not too late. Don't be too quick to give up." But when he recommended surgery, I firmly shook my head no. The doctor naturally urged me to think it over carefully, but simply just thinking it over seemed like too much trouble.

Even if I bet on a 60 percent chance and somehow survived, there would be a long rehabilitation period waiting for me. In some cases, multiple surgeries were necessary. I didn't have the strength to endure that. I couldn't see a future that was worth the suffering. Of course, there was also the problem of money. And, as for the remaining 40 percent chance, well, I didn't even want to imagine that outcome.

It was too much for me to focus on all of the issues in front of me, so day after day, I'd put off responding to the doctor.

And here was the result. Now that I could see my death taking shape and closing in on me, I was absolutely terrified. I started shaking violently. If there was one thing I couldn't face, this was it.

"The world is a fine place and worth the fighting for." I remembered what Ayako had said to me the first time I talked to her at the Torunka Café. If I fought back, what good would it do? Hemingway was supposed to be such a great writer, but what evidence did he base this idea on? What led him to write that?

"Let's put aside the issue of surgery for the moment and just get you checked into the hospital. Mr. Numata, if I'm not mistaken, you don't have a family—which is all the more reason why you should go through with it."

Although I'd refused his recommendations until now, this time my only option was to follow his orders.

What if I ended up collapsing at the Torunka? That would be serious. I couldn't put them in that situation. They were good people. I was just a guy who happened to walk in one day. There was no way I could impose on everyone in the café like that. I had to do what the doctor said. There was no other choice.

"How about three days from now? There's no need to rush into it. And we'll be able to make sure there's an open bed for you."

"Okay," I said, in my usual brusque way, then added quietly, "I'm in your hands."

It was clear that I'd caused too much trouble at the hotel where I'd been staying to remain there any longer. Once I'd packed everything into my single overnight bag, I was ready to move. I paid the bill and switched to an older, smaller hotel on the other side of the station.

How should I spend my last three days?

I thought it over in my gloomy hotel room. But I couldn't come up with anything in particular. There was only so much you could do in just three days, and if I made more memories there, it would simply make it harder to leave this place behind.

Still, I knew I should at least see Ayako and Tachibana to express my gratitude. I could tell them an appropriate lie, and perhaps I could even say that I was going away for a little while.

That way, they could all quickly forget about me. It might be better that way.

I slowly got up from my bed and headed down the same old backstreet.

"Ah, he's back!"

When I opened the door of the café, it was Tachibana's voice that I heard first.

"Ayako! Numata's back!"

From behind the counter, Tachibana gave his daughter a light reprimand. "Hey, Shizuku. You meant to say, 'Mr. Numata has returned.'"

"Yes, yes." Shizuku sighed.

"One yes will do."

"Enough already. This is why Kōta calls you the 'sister-in-law' behind your back."

"Who's a sister-in-law? Next time Kōta comes by, I won't let him get away with this."

Tachibana turned for help to the young man working for him part time. "Hey, Sylvie, will you say something to this stubborn girl?"

The young man answered right away, "What do you mean 'Sylvie'? Because of Shizuku now even the customers are starting to call me that."

"Hey, Sylvie, can I get another cup of coffee?"

"Look, this is all Shizuku's fault," the young man grumbled, aiming his comment in the direction of Old Mr. Takita.

A minute earlier, I'd been nervous to come, but once I was back in the usual bright atmosphere of the café, I suddenly felt relieved. But who on earth was Sylvie? I barely had time to think before I heard a voice call out to me from a table in the back.

"Oh, Hiro, you're finally here? Why didn't you come yesterday or the day before? I've been waiting for you."

I hadn't put in my order yet, but Tachibana was preparing a cup of the house blend for me. I went over to Ayako, who was waving me over, and sat down across from her.

"Sorry, I had some business to take care of."

"Is that right? Some mysterious business, huh? It's okay. Look at this though, ta-daaa!" Ayako said, sounding even more excited than usual as she spread some A4-size papers on the table. There were quite a few of them. I picked one up warily and saw it was a listing for an apartment to rent.

I looked back at Ayako, dumbfounded.

"I figured I'd pick out some places that looked good at the realtor's before you changed your mind. You've got a good friend, Hiro. Like they say, 'Friendship is a contract in which we undertake to exchange small favors for big ones.'"

Even though she said it like she was joking, I couldn't really laugh.

Over the past two days, I'd completely forgotten that the subject had ever come up. What was I thinking that day? And because of that impossible dream, I'd gotten Ayako all worked up over nothing...

"I love looking at floor plans. Isn't it kind of exciting? Let me know if you like any of them. There are a lot that you could get a tour of right now. And I have some time today too, so I could go with you if you like."

I sat there, unable to respond, and Ayako's cheerful expression suddenly darkened.

"What's wrong? You're not going to tell me you changed your mind, are you?"

"No, it's not that. Definitely not," I said, flustered. I didn't have it in me to reject Ayako's generous offer outright. Or rather, I didn't want to. "They all look so good," I said. "I can't make up my mind."

"I know, right? I got the ones that were brand-new apartment buildings that seemed right for you. The one I recommend is . . ."

I stared weakly at Ayako, who was talking excitedly with that glint in her eye again. After thinking over how I could divert her attention from the papers in front of us, I said, "Hey."

"What?"

"The weather's, um, nice today, isn't it?"

"Yeah, sure. But how about this apartment . . ."

"Hey."

"What?"

"The weather's nice today."

"I heard. So?"

"So, let's tour the places another time, and how about we go someplace today? You have time, right? I'm grateful that you found all these listings for me. I'll go over them carefully tonight." I offered this desperate suggestion in such a cheerful way that Ayako suspected something.

"That hardly sounds like you, Hiro," she said. "But I suppose you do have to think it over carefully to make a choice. So should we go for a walk, then, since you asked?"

Which is how the two of us ended up leaving the Torunka Café after 2:00 p.m. that day.

My plan had been to say a short goodbye and then make my escape, but I got swayed by her offer. I thought to myself, As long as I don't have another flare-up . . . That's the only thing I was worried about, and yet, at the same time, I felt elated. My heart was beating fast.

The Place Where We Meet Again

We walked with no particular destination. It was early summer already in Tokyo. Just walking in short sleeves, I could feel the sweat forming on my back. In part because it was the weekend, there were a lot of people out in the neighborhood; we even saw a group of foreigners who looked like tourists.

Ayako was walking ahead with a steady stride when she seemed to suddenly remember something. "By the way, Hiro," she asked, "have you recovered?"

"Yeah, I'm completely fine."

"Well, your complexion doesn't look so good, all things considered."

"That's what it's normally like."

"So you're saying your complexion is normally bad? That's concerning in and of itself."

"Anyhow, there's nothing wrong with me. The doctor said so. So you can depend on it."

"Hm, I hope so. Still, you gave me quite a shock that day. You hit the ground right in front of me. But that's how we got to know each other. Life is funny, isn't it?"

"I caused a lot of trouble for you that day," I said, trying to keep my composure as I hurried to keep up with Ayako, who was walking along with a spring in her step.

"If you're feeling better already, that's great," she said, sounding relieved. "But it's best not to push yourself too hard," she added with a smile.

She took me with her as she walked around, turning aimlessly in one direction or another. I suppose this was mostly what I expected when I decided to go with her. We avoided the main streets and took the backstreets. Whenever she saw a used-book store or a shop that drew her attention, she didn't hesitate to go in, and sometimes even ended up chatting with the person who ran the shop. I just went along, but it was a pleasure to watch her stroll down familiar streets like she was being carried along by the breeze.

When we got back to the market street, we stopped at a butcher shop that had a display of fried food and bought some deep-fried beef patties. Then we sat side by side on a bench nearby and dug in while they were still piping hot. We bit through the golden-brown exterior, releasing the juices inside. The flavor might not have been very sophisticated, but they were absolute perfection. "The patties here are delicious, aren't they?" Ayako said with a satisfied smile, her lips glinting with oil.

"They're great," I said, laughing.

A tame-seeming stray cat with black-and-white fur appeared out of nowhere and sat right in front of us, probably waiting for our leftovers. "Don't—if he eats that, he'll end up with diarrhea," she scolded me as I was about to give him a little piece. She opened her sketchbook and started to sketch the cat, who had just begun to groom himself.

While Ayako's pencil moved swiftly across the page, I sat beside her, staring off into the brilliant sunlight shining over the low buildings in front of us. When I closed my eyes, I could feel the light warming the back of my eyelids.

How peaceful, I thought. I wish it could stay like this forever.

I felt the feeling welling up inside me, then I quickly shook my head. There'd be no more days like this after today.

A little old woman, whom I'd often seen at the Torunka Café, was carrying shopping bags with a bunch of giant scallions sticking out of it. She called out cheerfully, "Oh, hello, Ayako!"

When Ayako greeted her with a friendly "Oh, hello, Chiyoko

Obāchan," the old woman even gave me a friendly little bow. I awkwardly bowed back.

After that, we stopped at a monjayaki place on the avenue at Ayako's request, since she apparently wasn't full yet, and by the time we left, the sun had nearly set. "Let's walk it off," Ayako said as she pulled me along with her, and we went all the way to Shinobazu Pond in Ueno Park.

We were a little tired from all the walking at that point, and so when we reached the pond, we sat down on a bench, facing the setting sun. The wind picked up then, blowing straight at us, making the leaves of the lotus flowers that covered the pond sway in the breeze.

The breeze felt good as it cooled my sweaty cheeks.

"Pretty, isn't it?" Ayako said with a touch of sadness in her voice as she took her sketchbook out of her bag again.

"You're right."

The sun was slowly but surely sinking in the sky, covering everything in a pale orange light. A young couple walked by. The sight of that couple circling the pond and the surface of the water lit up and shining in the setting sun looked like a picture ready to be framed.

"Sunsets like this make me think of my mother. She loved a good sunset too."

I snuck a glance at her. She was looking up at the sky, her eyes half closed, and her sketchbook resting on her knees. As the light of the setting sun shone on the side of her face, I could see Sanae's face overlaid on top of it, and my heart trembled.

"You know my mother used to say that when she watched the sun set, she'd think of that younger version of herself she'd left behind long ago. Tears would come to her eyes, and sometimes she'd start crying on her way home from shopping at the market. I was just a kid, and I couldn't figure out why she was crying. It just seemed strange to me. But now, I think I sort of understand what she was feeling."

Hearing those words coming from Ayako's lips, I was overcome by emotion.

What could Sanae have been thinking of as she stood in the middle of that busy market street with tears in her eyes? What was going through her head? So much time had passed, and we were now far apart. It was enough to make you burst out crying in public.

"I said something depressing again, didn't I?" Ayako was smiling, but I couldn't find the words to respond.

"What's wrong, Hiro?"

"I . . ." I murmured. "I was just remembering something from a long time ago."

"Hey, Hiro, you're quite the romantic."

Though Ayako meant to tease me with those words I'd heard so long ago, I ignored her and went on talking.

"There was someone I loved very much then. Someone I truly, truly loved."

Ayako turned to face me, then stared at me intently. "Hey, wow, and?"

"I abandoned her," I mumbled, looking down to avoid her eyes.

I heard her mutter "Hm?" as if she didn't understand. "Why? If she meant so much to you, then wouldn't you have wanted to stay together forever?"

"Even I don't understand how I could do something like that. I was a stupid kid. I couldn't conceive of anything that wasn't

The Place Where We Meet Again

right in front of me. I let myself be blinded by greed... When I came across an opportunity, it suddenly seemed like she was in the way."

"Tsk-tsk, it sounds like you must have been a self-centered man."

"You probably think I was the worst," I said.

Ayako responded with a wry smile. "Well, it's not earning you any praise. Do you regret it?"

"I regret it so much now that I think it might kill me. Whenever I think about what happened, I want to bash my head in. She was the one person I ever loved. And she was the only one who could've loved me like that. If I could, I'd get down on my knees and beg her to forgive me."

"Really... I hope that wherever she is, she's happy."

I couldn't look at her. I stared up into the darkening sky and nodded. "Yeah..."

"I'm sure she is happy, if you're really wishing for it. I'm sure she's long since forgotten those days, and she's living a very happy life, dancing in the streets like in a musical, *lalala-lala*. She's living a wonderful life." As she said this to me, she tried to comfort me by patting the back of my hand resting on the bench between us. The warmth of her touch made me want to cry again.

"Hiro, do you know this one?"

"Hmmm?"

"'A woman may be deceived by a hundred men, yet she will still fall in love with the hundred-first.' It's a line from a German poet. Human beings don't stop loving no matter how many times they get hurt. I think it's in our nature. So, it's okay for you to love again too. It doesn't have to be some sappy romance either. Love comes in many forms. There's the kind of love you feel for your family, the love for your friends, even for your job or your dreams—or the love for your pet, there's nothing wrong with that either. As long as you're not just dependent, and you can proudly call it love, the object of that love can be anything. Sometimes love can save you. And a life without any love at all would be lonely, don't you think?"

I stopped looking at the sky then and stared hard at Ayako. "You say some pretty incredible things. I've never had anyone in my life who would tell me something like that."

"Wait, are you complimenting me now?" Ayako asked the question with such a childlike smile on her face that I started to laugh a little.

"It's from the heart."

"I did it! I got a compliment from Hiro. Well, I might have said something that sounded wise, but the truth is I barely understand these things. And that goes for all the quotes I'm always running around collecting. When my father left us when I was six, I couldn't understand what had happened. What was life about? What do we live for? I thought there had to be some answers in these quotes from important people. There had to be some truth there. It's funny, you know. I was this elementary school kid mumbling quotes from Rousseau with a smug look on her face. But basically, I didn't know anything."

Ayako gave a little laugh, like she was trying to hide her embarrassment. Then she got up from the bench and said, "Should we get going?" The setting sun was now mostly hidden behind the jumbled row of buildings along the back edge of the pond, and only its final rays reached us. Giant clouds drifted across the

The Place Where We Meet Again

now deep blue sky. The breeze blowing across the surface of the water felt a little chilly.

"Hey, Ayako."

"Yeah?"

I'd thought it might be better to go our separate ways without saying anything more, but after all she'd done for me, it seemed ungrateful to leave like that. I couldn't expect her to forgive me. I took a deep breath and started to speak. "Actually, um, I've got to go away for a while."

"Away?"

"Yeah, for a little while. Overseas."

Ayako was standing in front of me, with a surprised look on her face. "Huh? When?"

"Tomorrow."

"Wait, what do you mean? That's so sudden. When are you coming back?"

"I'm not sure. But it'll be a long time." I looked down, trying to dodge the question. The expression on Ayako's face changed to something I'd never seen before. An anxious look, like she was frightened of something. I immediately regretted what I'd done, but it was too late.

"Is that right..."

"Sorry, it was hard for me to tell you."

"No, I'm sorry. It's because I was pressuring you to move, right? I think I sensed somehow that you might leave sooner or later. It just felt like that. And because we'd become friends, I didn't want you to go. I guess my intuition was right..."

I apologized again, still looking down at the ground. "Sorry."

"Why are you apologizing? You're coming back, aren't you? In that case, everything's fine. After all, I'm sure you have some mysterious business to take care of," Ayako said, forcing herself to be cheerful, after looking so troubled only a moment ago.

I couldn't speak, and she looked right at me and repeated what she'd said. "You are coming back, aren't you?"

I could feel her eyes staring intently at me, but I couldn't return her gaze.

That night, I had another dream.

"Hiro..."

When I turned to look, I saw Sanae in her old apartment. But this time she was the only one who still looked the same—I looked like a middle-aged man over fifty.

Everything else was the way it used to be. The view of the sunset from the window, the scent of the old tatami mats, the small low table, and Sanae kneeling with her legs folded neatly beneath her on that red cushion. I was the only thing that didn't fit. In that tiny room, I was the only one out of place.

"Sanae..."

I slowly stood up from my spot at the window and walked over to her. As she watched me from the corner of the room, her eyes narrowed into a smile.

I nearly fell to my knees in front of her. "Sanae..." I called her name again. The tears fell from my eyes. I couldn't stop myself from crying.

"What is it, Hiro?"

"I'm so sorry for what happened, Sanae. I was out of my mind. I...made a mistake. You were right. As long as we were together, everything was okay. I made a mistake. It was all a mistake..."

I bowed down, pressing my head to the floor, begging for forgiveness. Sanae gently put her hand on me. Her fingers were dyed the colors of the sunset.

"That's all over now. It happened so long ago. Over thirty years ago now."

"But I . . ."

"There's no 'but,'" Sanae said, her voice soft but definitive. "More importantly, though, what do you think of my daughter, Ayako? She's a good kid, isn't she?"

"Yeah, she's really special. She's kind and honest, and she's got a quick mind. She's a wonderful girl," I said, without stopping to wipe the tears from my eyes as I lay at her knees. Sanae laughed in that gentle, inviting voice.

"She does have a pretty reckless side to her that makes me worry though. But she's been through some difficult times. And I'm afraid I put her under a lot of strain. Especially with everything that happened with her father. That girl has always hungered for her father's love. I think maybe she sees you as a father figure."

"Me?" I said, looking up at her. I was taken aback. The thought had never occurred to me, and Ayako had never shown any sign of that to me.

"It's just a feeling I have. But anyway, you made her a promise, didn't you?"

"A promise?"

Sanae went on before I could comprehend what she meant.

"Already forgotten?" Sanae's face had the same annoyed look she had back then. "You told her you'd be coming back, didn't you? You better keep that promise. That girl truly cares about you. Don't let her down. You don't want to hurt her, do you?"

"But I . . ."

"You're okay. You're definitely going to be all right. Have I ever steered you wrong before?" Sanae said, sounding unusually confident.

I looked up at her and all I could do was shake my head. "No, you were always right. You always were."

"That's right." Sanae smiled one last time, her face lit up by the sunset. "Take care of yourself, Hiro. See you in another dream."

There, right in front of me, was my coffee, steam quietly rising from the white porcelain cup.

On my final evening, I went to the Torunka Café, carrying an overnight bag with all of my possessions stuffed inside. I was scheduled to be at the hospital for my surgery the next day, but they'd told me they could admit me as early as the evening before, so I was going to go straight there from the café. It would take me less than twenty minutes by train, yet it seemed impossibly far away.

I could feel my resolve weakening as I thought it over. I closed my eyes and inhaled the gentle aroma of my cup of coffee deep into my lungs.

It struck me then that this was my first time coming to the café at night. It was already past eight o'clock, and there were only two other groups of customers. Tonight, Tachibana was alone at the counter. Bathed in the amber light of the hanging lanterns, the café seemed even more serene than in the daytime.

The evening atmosphere wasn't too bad at all. I almost wished I'd discovered it sooner.

I opened my eyes, slowly reached for my last cup of coffee, and raised it to my lips. The rich flavor of the coffee beans filled my mouth, followed by a slight bitterness as it went down my throat. I felt the warmth gradually spread from my belly, like the glow of a lantern lit deep inside my stomach.

It was good. It really was good coffee. I wished I could have coffee this wonderful every day.

"The world is a fine place and worth the fighting for . . ."

I definitely wouldn't go that far. Life is hard to define. How could you force someone to see its value? But it just might be worth fighting for a cup of coffee like this. If it meant I could have coffee this good again, I might be able to go on fighting a little longer.

You made her a promise, didn't you? That's what Sanae had said. "Don't let her down."

I knew it was just a dream. It lasted a brief moment and only told me what I wanted to hear.

But even if it was just a dream, I didn't want to betray Sanae again. Or Ayako, of course. It was true. I had promised her.

So, I made a decision.

No more worthless hesitation or self-pity. I would do everything in my power. Once I'd made my decision, my heart felt much lighter.

"This is unusual for you. Coming at night," Tachibana said, as he took one glass at a time from the row on the counter and polished each one by hand.

"Yeah, I, um, just wanted to say goodbye," I said brusquely, while I savored each drop of my coffee.

Tachibana stopped polishing the glass in his hand and turned his attention to me.

"Goodbye?"

"I've got to go away for a bit. I won't be coming in for a while."

"Is that right? I'm sorry to hear that."

I knew that as long as I didn't say anything more, he wouldn't try to pry any further. I was deeply grateful for his discretion.

"You make a fine cup of coffee," I said. "And I've enjoyed talking to you."

It was my way of thanking him. He grinned from ear to ear.

"Thank you very much. I'll do my best to keep the place from going under before you return. So, please come again."

"I'd appreciate that. Say hello to your spirited daughter, and the cool young guy who works part time."

"I will."

"If I make it back okay..."

"Yes."

"Maybe you won't mind if I tell you my story next time. It's a long one, and it might be boring, but..."

"With pleasure."

We fell silent. The melody of the Chopin piece playing over the speakers sounded sweet to our ears, like the dream of some distant land. I listened carefully to the sound of the music, then drank the rest of my coffee and got up to leave.

I paid my bill, walked to the door, but as I grasped the brass knob, I paused.

I'll come back to this place again, no matter what happens. I'll have another cup of Tachibana's coffee. Once I became a better version of myself, I'd come back with my head held high.

I swear.

"Hey, Tachibana. The coffee you make here truly is the Devil's drink. And it seems I've fallen completely under its spell."

"There's no higher praise than that," Tachibana said, and gave me a polite bow.

When I got outside, the sky overhead was as dark as the coffee I'd just finished. And the small white crescent moon was hanging in the middle of it.

I had started down the narrow lane on my way to the station when someone suddenly called out to me.

"Hiro."

A familiar silhouette stepped into view under the dim white glow of the streetlights.

I was so taken aback that I shouted; my voice was too loud for that quiet little street. "Ayako, what are you doing here?"

I thought we'd already finished saying our goodbyes. I couldn't understand why she'd go out of her way to come see me again.

"I've been waiting for you," she said. "I was sure you'd be here today. There's something I want to give you."

"Something for me?"

"Let's walk together. You're going to the station, right?"

I followed her without knowing what was going on. The street ahead of us, lit by the faint light of the moon, was so quiet it seemed forlorn. I was glad that Ayako had come to see me.

Rather than turning off the market street, Ayako took the long way that led through Yanaka Cemetery. It would still take us fifteen minutes at most to reach the station in Nippori.

We walked side by side down the long, straight path that led to the station, bordered the whole way by cherry trees thick with green leaves.

Halfway through the cemetery, she suddenly stopped and took something out of her bag. She held it out for me to take.

"Here."

At first I thought it was a note, but I was wrong. It was a photograph. Before I knew it, I was standing under a streetlight examining it carefully.

"That's you, isn't it?" Ayako said casually. I looked at her, and then I turned back to the photo, disconcerted.

It was definitely me in the photograph. There we were, Sanae and me together, back when we were young. We were nestled against each other by the window in that old apartment. You could see the orange light of the sunset outside the window.

I remembered that day. The photograph was taken a few months before I left her. It was from a period when our relationship was the closest it ever was. Sanae had borrowed a single reflex camera from a coworker at the cleaner's and insisted we take a picture together. So we used the self-timer to take our picture with the sunset in the background. Sanae didn't even know how to put in the film. I was the one who taught her how to adjust the focus and the exposure. For the next month, Sanae was constantly taking pictures, but I was too embarrassed, and kept making excuses, and in the end, I never saw any of the photos that were developed.

We're slightly backlit, so it was a little hard to make out our expressions. Sanae is facing the camera and seems to be smiling. I, on the other hand, am staring in the wrong direction with a sour look on my face. In some ways, the photograph reflects our personalities and our relationship at the time. The two people in the photograph were extraordinarily young, and amazingly carefree. They had absolutely no fear of what was to come.

"Where did you . . . ?"

"It used to be in my mother's album. It is you, isn't it? Yes, you're much older now, but when I compare the face in the picture to yours, I can definitely see a resemblance."

"How long have you known?" Of course, I had no memory of talking to Ayako about any of this. I was afraid of how she might react, and so, in the end, I never discussed it. And yet . . .

"I had no idea until recently," she said. "The day before yesterday, when you were talking about the past, I just had this feeling I couldn't shake."

"Ayako, I—"

Ayako interrupted me then and went on talking.

"Back when I was in middle school, I think, I started wondering if we still had any pictures left of my father. I was digging through a drawer when I came across that picture. I was surprised so I asked my mother about it. She seemed embarrassed and asked me where I'd dug up that picture. Before she married my father, she'd thrown away everything related to her old boyfriend, but for some reason, she couldn't get rid of that picture. She said there were a lot of memories in that photograph. It meant a great deal to her."

Ayako peered at the photograph in my hand. "It really is a good picture," she said, nodding. "I only looked at it that one time, but it made a strong impression on me. I didn't realize it for a long time after we met, but I always felt frustrated whenever I saw you, and then the other day, it finally hit me. He's the guy in the photo! Once I'd solved the mystery, I felt so much better."

Then she pulled me by the sleeve. "Come on," she said, "let's walk." I got ahold of myself at last and chased after her as she headed off into the green landscape of the cemetery.

Ayako turned to me and smiled. "You can have the picture. I don't need it. And I think my mother would be happier if you had it."

"Ayako."

"Yes?"

"I..."

"You don't have to say anything. I didn't bring it to interrogate you. I just thought it might give you luck on your long trip. The last time we talked I got the sense that you might not be coming back. But if you have this with you, I think you'll be okay."

"Thank you." My voice sounded hoarse—they were not words I was accustomed to saying. But when I said it to Ayako, it conveyed a thousand different feelings. Ayako just smiled back. It would've been perfectly understandable to expect an explanation, but she didn't ask for one. She knew that I wouldn't want to explain.

Sanae, your daughter really is wonderful. It hurts to say goodbye to her. As tough as I am, I have tears in my eyes.

When we came to the brightly lit overpass that led to the gates of the station, Ayako rummaged around in her bag again. This time she brought out something that looked like a postcard. "And this is from me," she said.

It was a drawing she'd made. It showed the face of a man who looked familiar. Unlike her pencil drawings I'd seen in the past, she'd also added watercolors to this one.

"Is this ... me?"

"It is. You asked me to draw you before, didn't you? I drew you from memory, so it might not look too much like you. And I wanted to draw you smiling, but you rarely smile, so the face was kind of tricky."

In the picture, she drew me facing straight ahead, with an awkward smile on my face. Behind me, the background was filled by a pale pink flower that looked like a cloud dyed the color of the sunset.

"A middle-aged guy and a flower. Quite the odd couple," I said, trying to hide my embarrassment. But I couldn't keep my voice from trembling.

"It's a Hardenbergia. In the language of flowers, it's a symbol of 'miraculous reunions.' I painted it in the hope that we'll meet again someday. It'll help watch over you, though maybe not as much as the picture with my mother. Hey, don't cry. It's nothing special."

"I'm not crying. That's impossible."

"I get it. You're not crying. You're definitely not crying." I thought Ayako would laugh then, but her voice grew quiet. "Thank you for everything, Hiro. I had fun with you."

"I'm the one who ought to be saying thank you. I knew about you from way before. I'd been wanting to talk to you the whole time."

"No. I'm the one. It was only for a brief moment, but it felt sort of like I was with my father. I didn't mention it because I didn't want to make you mad at me."

"Aren't you saying it now?"

"You've got good ears." Ayako gave me a punch in my arm that felt like she really meant it. But even that pain felt like tenderness now.

"Hey, how about one last quotation?"

"Another?" I said with a wry smile. How on earth was I supposed to cram another quote from some great figure into my brain?

"'In life, reunions are the closest thing we get to miracles.'"

"Who said that?" I asked, quickly wiping away a tear that had fallen on my cheek, hoping Ayako hadn't noticed—though it was probably too late.

"That was one of mine. I just came up with it. But I really believe it. It comes from the heart."

"It's a good one," I said. "It's my favorite so far."

Ayako grinned.

We stood there looking at each other for a while. We didn't say a word—we just looked at each other. There were things I wanted to tell her. So many things. But they were caught in my throat, and they wouldn't come out. I felt that if I tried to force them, they might come out as something different from what I meant to say. So I didn't say anything.

There was a low rumble as a train passed beneath the overpass where we were standing.

Ayako gave me one last smile, then turned and ran off down the path we'd just taken.

"Take care! Let's get coffee together again! With lots of milk!"

"You should always take your coffee black. There's no other way!"

"Stubborn as ever!"

Even after Ayako disappeared into the darkness, I remained standing there under the lights at the entrance to the station, holding those two treasures in my hands.

May her life from this day forward be filled with happiness. That's what I wished for.

I'll dream of the day when the two of us can have coffee together again at the Torunka Café.

In life, reunions are the closest thing we get to miracles. I said the words softly to myself.

There was no doubt about it. She said it, so it must be true.

I took a deep breath and passed through the gates of the station, leaving behind this place of memories I'll never let go.

Part Three

A Drop of Love

My father was the one who named me Shizuku.

I asked him once when I was little about the origin of my name.

"I gave you that name because I hoped you'd turn out like coffee," he said. "To make a good cup of coffee you need to devote your attention to extracting the flavor from the beans. If not, you won't bring out the rich aroma and deeper flavors. But if you do it right, it means that every drop of coffee in the cup will have that concentrated flavor. What I wanted for you was that your life would be as rich and satisfying."

Weird, isn't it? What did he mean by "extracting"? At the same time though, the story behind my name seemed so like my dad that I remember I felt strangely satisfied by his explanation.

My dad started running the Torunka Café before I was born.

It sits all by itself at the end of a narrow dead-end street, a little shop capped with a triangular roof. There are five tables near the window, and six stools at the counter. The window, set in a drab brick wall, is stained glass, and the tables and chairs are all made of wood.

He took it over from the old woman who owned the café first, so the interior and exterior are both pretty old.

Sir. The customers called my father *sir.*

"Give me a blend, sir."

"An ice coffee for me, sir."

Of course, when I was young, I didn't understand what it meant, but I somehow sensed that the people who called him "sir" were showing how much they respected him, and it made me feel strangely proud.

For me, my father was a man who stood behind that counter every day, making coffee with this delicious aroma but hardly saying a word. And he always had this serious look on his face. With a father like that, I guess it should come as no surprise that I was named after coffee.

Given who my father was and the fact that my name was connected to coffee, it makes sense that there might be some confusion with all the talk about the flavor of the coffee. The customers would say things to me like, "So the owner uses cloth drip filters here? The aftertaste is totally different."

But the truth is, I never drink coffee. All in all, it's been nearly ten years since I've touched the stuff. The last time I had some was right after I started elementary school. I hated it right from the first taste, and I still do. So I have no idea what difference it makes if you use a cloth filter or paper filter.

That's because the night I drank coffee, I had a terrible nightmare.

Having grown up surrounded by people who loved coffee from the time I was little, I'd always longed to taste it for myself. People looked like they were enjoying it so much that I knew it had to be unbelievably delicious. But no matter how much I begged my father, he refused to let me have any. "You're too young," he always said.

My sister was the one who gave me coffee. She was six years older and had a mature air about her. She'd started drinking coffee before she entered middle school. One day, while I was going on and on complaining, my sister secretly passed me the cup of coffee my father had made for her. "I understand the urge to try it," she told me, "but you're not ready yet."

My father was behind the counter, but I took a big gulp from the cup while his back was turned. The only impression I had of the flavor was how bitter it was. Privately, I felt let down by the fact that this was what all those adults had been drinking like it was so delicious. "Hey, don't force yourself." My sister laughed. "I'll drink the rest." But that only fired up my competitive side, so I endured the bitterness in my throat and my queasy stomach, and drank the remaining half of the black liquid in that cup, right down to the last drop.

"It was delicious," I said, trying my best to look tough as I grimaced.

"You might not be able to sleep tonight," my sister said, taking back the empty cup and looking at me with pity.

"What? Why?"

"Coffee has a little something called caffeine in it that makes people feel excited. In some cases, people who aren't used to it can feel overstimulated. And when that happens, they can't sleep. That was your first coffee, wasn't it, Shizuku? And you just turned seven. I hope you're all right."

"What? Is that true? Why didn't you tell me sooner?" I said, in a hurry to blame my sister. My sister had been a bookworm since she was little and now knew all sorts of things. So when she gave me that warning calmly and patiently, I got incredibly worried. And whether it was because of the power of suggestion or the actual effects of caffeine, right as we were talking about it I started to feel my head spin like it was locked inside a washing machine.

"What should I do?"

"There's nothing you can do. You already drank it." She sounded somewhat sympathetic, but then she shrugged, and said, "It's your own fault."

The night went just as I'd feared. I was wide awake—never in my life had I felt so alert—and though I must have tossed and turned dozens of times, I never felt the least bit sleepy. The house was terribly quiet and still. You couldn't hear a sound. It was like I'd fallen into the depths of the night. I was terrified.

At some point, as my eyelids opened and closed over and over, I realized I was walking outside. Except it wasn't the market street that I knew so well that I could identify the shops without looking. Now all the buildings looked like melting blocks of cheese, and there was not a single person around. The streetlights kept flickering, and as I walked barefoot in my pajamas, the shadow I cast grew larger until it took on a terrifying, demonic shape on the road behind me.

I need to get home. I dragged myself forward; my body felt as heavy as lead as I wandered around the utterly transformed market street. But the little lane by the grocer that should've led to our house had vanished. In its place, a perfectly white wall, the color of the coffee cup I'd drunk from that afternoon, was towering over me. The wall was eerily cold, and it wouldn't budge no matter how much I pushed or banged on it.

What can I do? I can't get home. I won't make it out of this twisted world alive.

I felt so hopeless I started to sob. If only I hadn't had that cof-

A Drop of Love

fee! I never should've let it touch my lips. Oh, please, God, please bring me back to the safe world I know.

Then someone shook me awake, and I was in my room again. Somehow it was already morning. The rays of morning sunlight were shining through the opening in the curtains.

I was trembling like a fish on dry land. I think I must've been moaning in my sleep.

"Hey, Shizuku, are you all right?"

Even after I heard my mother's voice as she peered into my room, I just stayed there in a daze. It must've been a dream. But where did it come from? When did I fall asleep? Although everything was still hazy, I clung to my mother and sobbed, relieved that I had made it back safe and sound.

After that, they found out that I'd had coffee, and my father gave me a severe scolding. "From now on," he told me, "you are forbidden to drink coffee," but I didn't need to be told that—I couldn't stand the sight of it.

That's why I've only had coffee that one time. I'm sure now that I'm in high school, I won't get nightmares like that again. But just in case. I never want to experience another vivid and bizarre dream like that. I don't want to slip back into that strange world again. Even just thinking about it sends a chill down my spine.

"So that's the reason why you hate coffee, Shizuku. It's really fascinating."

It was another peaceful afternoon at the Torunka Café. After listening to my story, Chinatsu seemed thoroughly impressed. I'd only meant to make small talk, but her reaction went so far beyond what I'd expected that I felt a little embarrassed.

The long rainy season had ended, and now, at the end of July, summer was in full swing. Outside the window, there were white clouds like puffs of smoke floating in a sky so uniformly blue that you suspected it had been freshly painted. The days of endless rain had vanished right when my high school's summer break began, and now every day was sunny and clear.

Starting with Ayako, the illustrator who lived in the neighborhood, all of the customers who had stuck with hot coffee this far switched their orders, one after the other, to iced coffee, and now it was really only Chinatsu who still ordered her coffee hot.

"But the story behind your name is really wonderful, Shizuku. A life as rich and satisfying as coffee—that's so like your father," Chinatsu said, glancing at him across the counter as she raised the cup to her lips.

My father kept silently polishing the glasses as if he hadn't heard her. I was worried he'd get carried away if he heard himself being complimented by a pretty girl, so I didn't share it with him. Instead, I tried to steer us back to the topic we were supposed to be discussing.

"What was it you wanted my advice about?"

We'd met up for coffee today because Chinatsu had told me she wanted to ask me for my advice about something. Chinatsu was one of our regulars, a quiet, shy girl who was also very pretty. She reminded me a little of my sister. Though, of course, that wasn't the only reason why I really liked her. I would've been happy to give her advice about anything at all.

"I actually wanted to ask you about Shūichi."

"Wait, Shūichi?"

She nodded, looking quite serious.

"Well, if it's about Shūichi, I'm sure you know him a lot better than I do," I said with a grin.

Chinatsu looked thoroughly embarrassed. She was pulling on her bangs the way she always did.

"No, um, I . . . how can I put it? I'm not sure what to do."

"Ooh, about what?" I leaned across the table, my curiosity piqued. Chinatsu and Shūichi, who worked part time at the café, had met in dramatic fashion at the end of last year, and though I don't know all the details of the story, they were now the Torunka Café's official couple. Chinatsu didn't normally tell me much about Shūichi because it made her embarrassed, so this was a rare treat.

"Next month is his birthday, right? And I want to give him a present, but I don't know what to get him."

"Wait, is that what this is about? Hmmm . . . Shūichi's a summer baby? That doesn't fit my idea of him at all."

Chinatsu laughed quietly. "That's true. It's not exactly the impression he gives off."

Shūichi had been so busy lately that he'd been taking a lot of time off from working at the Torunka. Thanks to all the effort he put into his job search, he managed to land an informal offer in an editorial production department, so he was spending the summer training there part time. All this was, without a doubt, Chinatsu's influence. It wasn't long ago that he'd declared he'd be happy to be a student for the rest of his life.

"But I'm getting worried that he's pushing himself too hard," Chinatsu said, looking terribly worried. "It could be bad for his health. So I really want to get him something nice to make him happy." From the look on her face, I could see how much she loved Shūichi. As I sipped my ginger ale, I thought to myself, So this is what love looks like.

"I see," I said, holding back my urge to smirk and laugh. "Shūichi, hmmm . . . he tends to like older things. Would you say he's into vintage things? Like he probably collects vinyl records. And he likes the café so much he got a job here."

"That's true. I was thinking something along those lines might be good, but I don't know much about that sort of thing. There are a lot of vintage stores in this neighborhood that sell, right? Do you know a good place?"

"Hmmm," I mumbled, chewing on my straw. I could find a bunch of places that girls my age would like, but we were talking about Shūichi here, who was already fully an old-man-in-waiting. I had no idea which spot would make him happy.

"Okay, how about we go look together next Sunday? I know most of the places around here, so I can at least help you find them."

"You wouldn't mind?"

"Of course not. Besides, I could never refuse a request from you. Plus, for my birthday in May, Shūichi gave me a bookstore gift card, so I need to return the favor."

"Well, then let's do it." I could tell from the look on her face then that she was in love. Love must be amazing, I thought, to bring about such a wonderful smile.

"Wonderful." The moment the thought occurred to me, I realized I had said it aloud.

"What is?" Chinatsu looked back at me, confused.

"Oh, no, I just meant, it's wonderful to have someone you love." As I said those words, I got embarrassed and started laughing.

"There isn't a boy you like?"

The question caught me by surprise, which only made me laugh more.

"No way. Absolutely not. Lately, that's all the girls in class ever talk about. It's getting to be a bit of a problem, actually."

"But what about that boy who was your childhood friend?"

"You mean Kōta? No way. Absolutely not." I refuted that one right away after I'd nearly spit out the ice cube I'd been rolling around on my tongue.

"But Shūichi told me, 'Kōta's always making moves on Shizuku.'"

"Definitely not. He's just joking when he does that. It's his way of saying hi. He doesn't really mean it." It seemed like he was giving people the wrong impression.

My relationship with Kōta wasn't like that at all. We were truly just childhood friends. Our houses were only five minutes away from each other, and our parents were good friends, which meant we'd been together from kindergarten through high school. We were playing together when we were still in diapers, and in grade school we saw each other every morning when we walked together with the other kids in our group going to school. We basically grew up as siblings. As you'd expect, at this age we weren't together every day anymore, but aside from my family, he was the person I was closest to in the whole world. But that's really all there was to it. Besides, Kōta was pretty much an idiot. He was better than me at school, but deep down he was an idiot. That side of him made me laugh, so I liked him, but what I felt was a million light-years away from love.

I tried desperately to explain all this to her, but Chinatsu didn't seem entirely convinced. Just as I was trying to think of something that might show just how unromantic our relationship was...

"Wow, is it cold out there! Oh hey, boss."

Speak of the devil. The bell on the door jingled, and in came Kōta. It was summer break, so I knew he'd definitely slept in till noon. His bedhead hair made him look like a scientist whose experiment had just exploded. He seemed sleepy, and he was acting like even more of an idiot than usual. The atmosphere of the café, which had been filled with the sound of people quietly talking to each other, was now ruined.

"Kōta . . ." Right away, I heard the voice of my father, who detested that sort of sloppiness. "If you're going to visit a person's place of business, can't you at least get properly dressed?"

"Huh? What do you mean?" Kōta looked himself up and down, from his T-shirt to the pair of long shorts and sandals he was wearing. "These are my regular clothes," he said, without a hint of shame. Then he let out an absurdly big yawn. Unbelievable. Who on earth was going to fall for a guy like this? I'd be more likely to fall in love with a chimpanzee.

"Kōta, looks like summer vacation's making you lazy."

"Oh, Shizuku, you're here."

Just as my father was preparing to lecture him, Kōta deftly sidestepped it by coming over to me. He was the only one who could get away with treating my father that way at the café.

"Hey, don't come any closer!" I said, but Kōta forced his way through, ignoring my protests and sitting his butt down right beside me.

"What? Don't be embarrassed. Oh, I get it, you've finally fallen for me."

Before he'd finished saying those words, I gave him a swift smack in the head.

A Drop of Love

"That hurts, dummy. Don't do that in front of Chinatsu," he groaned, rubbing his bed head.

"You're the king of the dummies. You just woke up, didn't you!"

"I've been up for a long time."

"Well, you let out a yawn so big you nearly dislocated your jaw."

"So you were watching me the whole time?"

"No, you blithely walked into my field of view."

"Hey, Shizuku, stop messing around with that idiot and get back to work," my father interjected with a disgusted look on his face.

A picture's worth a thousand words. And this one saved me the trouble of having to explain the whole thing in detail. I turned to Chinatsu and said, "So, you see, there's no way I could have feelings for him."

Chinatsu nodded her head in agreement, looking astonished. "But the two of you are really close, and that's wonderful." She sounded so earnest that Kōta and I looked at each other and burst out laughing.

The idea of me falling in love with someone... When I tried to imagine it, it just didn't seem real. It was something that might happen in the distant future. But for now it seemed as far away as the day when I would drink coffee again.

"The anniversary of her death is coming, you know."

My father uttered those words that night as I was helping him clean up after closing.

"Hm?"

I stopped wiping the table and turned to look at him. He was standing at the register, calculating the day's proceeds.

The period right after closing always felt a little lonely. It got so quiet that it was unsettling. The feeling was even more intense now because my father always spoke about this subject in a whisper.

In the past, I used to be happy when we closed because that's when family time began. But now it was reversed. I longed for the time only a half hour earlier when our customers were still there. The end of the day was now the time I hated the most.

"This year is the sixth anniversary of her death, so I think we'll hold it at the temple."

"Oh, okay. Sure." I nodded as I watched the hanging lamp sway in the weak breeze of the air conditioner.

"We don't have to go overboard. We'll just invite some relatives and have the priest recite a sutra for her. Then we can all eat together after."

"Okay. Did you tell Mom?"

"I did. You think I'd forget something like that?"

"I guess not."

My mom was living abroad because of the circumstances. It was a pretty remote place, so we often couldn't get in touch with her. But it was something we were trying not to worry too much about.

"Is everyone going to be dressed in mourning clothes?"

"That's the plan. It's the six-year anniversary, after all. I felt bad about asking everyone to dress in mourning in the middle of summer, so I told our relatives to wear whatever they liked, but your aunt Mitsuko was vehemently against it."

"We hardly ever see her, but when it comes to something like this, she's got to find fault with everyone. She has to butt in and say, 'Oh, it sets a bad example,' and like, 'You'll bring shame upon the family,'" I said, imitating my aunt Mitsuko's way of talking, shrugging my shoulders in her affected way.

"It's fine. I'm just grateful to them for agreeing to come all this way. Don't let them see you pouting when they're here."

"Fine, I get it."

Socializing with our relatives was a real pain. How could they understand our grief? And all they cared about was following tradition and keeping up appearances. They even spoke ill of my mother, who was living apart from us, though they didn't understand the reasons why. They didn't understand anything. The more I thought about it, the angrier I became. I could feel it welling up from the pit of my stomach.

My father, who seemed to sense that by looking at me, said from the other side of the counter, "It's okay. What matters is that we understand."

His voice didn't have its usual stern tone. It's like he was trying to reason with me gently.

"Okay." I nodded meekly and told my father goodbye and went up to the second floor. I stepped out onto the veranda to breathe some fresh air and maybe calm my thoughts. Once I'd lit the mosquito coil with a match, I leaned back against the railing to relax.

Though it's in Tokyo, night comes early to this part of downtown.

It was still before ten. Though everyone wasn't necessarily asleep in the houses nearby, the whole area seemed engulfed in a silence so deep that it was like a spell had been cast over the neighborhood. Down on Torunka Street, our name for the narrow backstreet that led to the café, each streetlight cast a lonely light. An unidentified black object darted down the street—probably a stray cat. As I leaned back against the railing without moving, I felt the lukewarm breeze against my cheek, still carrying the warmth of the afternoon.

The stars were twinkling faintly in the black sky above. Without meaning to, my eyes searched for the Summer Triangle. I remembered the names of the stars my sister had taught me such a long time ago.

Deneb, Altair, Vega.

It sort of sounds like a magic spell. When my sister had heard me say that, she'd chuckled a little. She'd taught me their names like she was letting me in on a special secret.

Hey, Big Sister.

I tried talking to her in my head.

What's it like over there?

How are you?

Mom and Dad and I are doing fine down here. It was another peaceful day in Yanaka. You know everyone's so kind and funny in the neighborhood.

Hey, can you believe it?

I've caught up to you. I'm as old as you now. But I don't seem to be turning out much like you. I mean, I still can't drink coffee. And I've never been in love. When you were seventeen, you seemed so grown up, so why am I so different?

I kept looking up at the sky, but the stars only shined dimly overhead.

I was meeting Chinatsu in the morning before the sun got too strong. Even still, as we stood in front of the station, the sunlight beat down on us. We could hear the piercing sound of the large brown cicada coming from the direction of Yanaka Cemetery, which was surrounded in a deep green.

"The cicadas are unbelievable today, aren't they?"

Chinatsu was wearing a cute outfit again. A pale blue summer sweater with a long, lace skirt. Even on a hot day like this, there was something cool and refreshing about her. It was the kind of girlish outfit that I could never pull off.

I thought about how much the way she dressed reminded me of my sister. I felt a little ache pass through my chest. Like always. It happened whenever I saw an older girl who looked the slightest bit like my sister, whether it was her physique, her clothes, her voice, or just the feeling she gave off. I'd find myself searching for some resemblance in strangers I passed on the street. Then I'd start to imagine. If my sister had lived to this age, would she have turned out like this? Or would she be like that?

It was senseless and childish.

"Is anything wrong?" Chinatsu looked perplexed as I stood there in front of the station, making no attempt to move on.

"Oh no, nothing at all. Shall we go?"

We passed through the cemetery, which the season had transformed into a festival of cicadas, then we went down Sansakizaka. The antique shops and stores were scattered around the narrow lanes nearby, so we needed to find an efficient way to get around to see them, or we wouldn't make it in the heat. As a girl who grew up in the neighborhood, this was my time to shine. Over there was the place that sold cat-themed merchandise, and here was the store that specialized in decorative chiyogami paper. We went around the neighborhood checking out the stores, including those unusual shops. We'd walk a little and pop into a shop, check out the goods, then walk a little more up the hill, which, in the distance, seemed to shimmer in the heat. I took her to every shop I could think of, stopping for a break at a dessert shop for some sweet, refreshing anmitsu.

Just as we were huffing and puffing our way up the slope of Dangozaka, we ran into a group of grade-school boys who looked like they were on their way to the local pool. Despite the fact that true summer was still ahead of us, they were all already deeply tanned. Kōta's little brother, Yōhei, was with them. He started calling out, "It's Shizu! It's Shizu!" I gave his head a little chop, and said, "Show a little respect." His face and his cheeky attitude were exactly like Kōta's when he was little.

In the end, Chinatsu bought a canvas bag from a guy on Yomise Street who only shows up on the weekends, a sort of roving bag vendor. The bag was made of canvas, and it looked simple and durable. There was no doubt that Shūichi would like it too. It seemed like something he could use at work too. I bought a change purse from the same place.

"Thank you for everything today. You were a big help, and you made it a fun day." We'd succeeded in getting our shopping done without too much trouble, but I didn't know what to do when Chinatsu told me again how grateful she was. I said it was nothing, but she insisted.

"It's not just today. You always make me feel better. It really helps me. You're so good at cheering people up. It must be something you were born with. It's amazing, honestly."

She said it all with her usual earnestness, and because I'm terrible at accepting praise, I could feel my lower back getting itchy.

"Um, Chinatsu, maybe then I could ask you a favor in return?"

"What might that be? If there's anything I can do for you, I'm only too happy to help," she said with an anxious look on her face.

"Can you maybe not speak so politely to me? You're older than me, after all, and I'm not big on formality. You told me before that you couldn't speak without being so polite, but I want you to be more relaxed with me. I mean, we're friends, aren't we?" I said with a grin.

Chinatsu blushed almost imperceptibly and gave a little smile back.

"All right then, shall we go back to the Torunka?"

"Yes, I mean, um, yeah."

Then the two of us started walking down the avenue, headed for the market street, under a clear blue sky—and that's when it happened.

A young man in a white T-shirt and black glasses was headed our way. He passed us as we were happily chatting away.

As he passed us, I turned around all of a sudden. I had a sudden premonition. It felt like someone was tugging my hair from behind.

"Shizuku?" Chinatsu was right next to me, calling my name.

The man continued walking down the street with the summer sun blazing down on him. For some reason, I sensed he would turn around. As I was staring at him, he stopped walking and stood about three meters away.

And then slowly, he turned back toward me.

We locked eyes for a moment. And then he took a step in my direction and looked at me even more intently.

"Are you by any chance Shizuku?"

"Yeah..."

When I heard his voice, I was finally sure.

"Ogino?" The moment I said this, he came hurrying over to me. Behind his glasses his eyes were smiling with joy.

"It is you, Shizuku. It's been so long. You've grown up."

It was so sudden that I didn't have time to process what I was feeling. Unable to speak, I just stared back at him standing right in front me.

It really was Ogino. He'd been my sister's boyfriend. Then my sister died, and since then we'd abruptly lost contact with him.

To be honest, I'd completely forgotten he even existed until that very moment. Though the fact that I felt a premonition the moment we passed each other might be proof that deep down I hadn't forgotten him entirely.

"Is this your friend, Shizuku?"

I must've been trembling. Until he spoke those words, I'd forgotten Chinatsu was standing right next to me.

"Yeah, um, kind of."

Ogino gave her a little bow. Chinatsu bowed in return.

"Oh, um, would it be better if I went ahead to the Torunka? I mean, want me to go ahead?"

"Oh, um . . ."

I glanced at Ogino, unsure what to do.

"Oh, please don't let me interrupt your plans," he said. He seemed like he was ready to say "So long, Shizuku" and walk off.

But I heard myself call out to him as he was turning away. "Wait!"

The Mori Ōgai Memorial Museum is located on Dangozaka hill. The adjoining café on the grounds of the museum had a very sophisticated atmosphere. It was built with a glass wall that let you

A Drop of Love

look out at the garden as you drank your tea. In the corner of the garden was a large ginkgo, and it felt good to watch the beautiful, fresh green leaves stirring in the wind.

"There's something I want to talk to you about," I told him.

"In that case," he said, "let's go to the Mori Ōgai Museum." At first, I couldn't figure out why he wanted to go to the museum. I had no idea it had such a nice café.

"This is a great place."

The location had originally been the site of the writer Mori Ōgai's residence. The museum had been constructed relatively recently, and since I only knew his name from my modern lit class, the place had meant nothing to me until this moment.

"Isn't it? I like how relaxing it is."

As we sat together, Ogino kept looking at me and smiling. He didn't even bother to glance out the window at the big, beautiful garden. I sat there bewildered as he watched me with a sweet look on his face, the way an adult devotes their attention to a small child.

Oh, I realized, he's totally treating me like I'm a little kid.

No matter how old I got, his first impression of me would probably always be that I was the much younger sister of the girl he used to love. But if you think about it, I was now actually only one year younger than my sister had been the last time we saw each other. Ogino himself was in high school then. If I seemed like a little kid to him in those days, I guess, that's natural, but it didn't seem right for him to treat me like that now.

Although I knew that there was no way I could erase his impression of me, I tried to sound as grown up as possible.

"I really ought to apologize for calling out to you and forcing you to stop like that. I hope it wasn't too rude of me."

"Not at all. I'm off from work today, and didn't have any plans besides going to a used bookshop I like. But what about you? Weren't you with a friend?"

"It's fine. We'd finished our errand."

Chinatsu had gone ahead to the Torunka maybe because she sensed there was something peculiar about my relationship with Ogino. But there was no time to explain it to her then. I felt like if I'd let Ogino walk away at that moment, I'd never see him again.

"Oh, well, that's good, then. Still, it really has been such a long time. It must be six years since we last saw each other. How have you been? I guess you're in your second year of high school now, right?"

Ogino was still smiling at me as he took a sip of his iced coffee. As it went down his throat, his Adam's apple rose and fell noticeably. It was like an independent creature. I couldn't help staring at it.

Back then, he gave off the impression that he was delicate, even fragile. Now his shoulders and neck seemed pretty sturdy. The arms sticking out of his white shirt were slim but muscular. The boyishness had disappeared from his face, which now seemed quite manly. Looking him over, you could sense his mature composure. Would Kōta turn out like this in six or seven years? Nope. Totally impossible. The two of them were made of different stuff.

Ogino then and Ogino now. On the inside I was shocked by all the little ways he'd changed, but as I reached for my iced tea, I pretended like it was nothing.

"I've been doing fine, as always. How about you, Ogino? How have you been?"

"I'm fine. I was in Kyoto for college, and last year, I came back to Tokyo to get a job."

"Is that right?"

"How are your parents? Are they still running the café?"

"Yes."

"Oh, I haven't been to the Torunka Café in such a long time." Ogino's eyes narrowed as he said this, like he missed the old days.

"I'd meant to go say hello as soon as I got back, but it was difficult, you know."

"Why?"

"I was so awful to all of you."

"Awful?" I said. I truly had no idea what he was talking about. Had he done something to us? I couldn't think of anything.

"I mean, I was wailing at the funeral. And then I clung to the coffin. I lost it. I can't believe I went that far."

"No, we didn't get . . ."

Ogino quietly shook his head, and then shifted his gaze to the scenery out the window.

"It was inexcusable. You were the ones grieving, and then I come in, a guy who got dumped six months before, and start acting like that. Afterward, I realized how selfish I'd been, and then I felt truly terrible about it. I haven't been able to face your father ever since. I ought to have gone to see him before I left for college. He did so much for me."

"Please forget all of that. It really didn't bother us at all. To be honest, we didn't even have the emotional capacity at the time to pay much attention to you at all . . ."

I never knew he felt that way. I'd just assumed that the reason he never came to see us was because he didn't want to revisit those sad memories.

"Please come back to the café sometime, if you ever feel like it. My father would be thrilled."

My father liked Ogino, even aside from the fact that he was my sister's boyfriend. There was no doubt about it. He'd be thrilled.

"Really? He wouldn't mind?"

"Of course not."

"Well, then maybe I'll pay him a visit sometime soon."

Ogino grinned. His smile was warm and pleasant.

"Um, do you mind if I ask you something?" I said, taking advantage of that smile to bring up a difficult topic. "Why did you and my sister break up?"

They had split up after going out less than a year, despite the fact that everyone was always saying they seemed like such a great match. It didn't feel right to ask him about it now, but if I didn't, I'd never be able to make sense of it.

"Oh that."

Ogino's smile seemed to waver for a moment, but he quickly regained his composure. I pretended I hadn't noticed.

"I was the one who got dumped. She said, 'I'm breaking up with you because I like someone else.'"

"So that's how it happened . . . Is that why she kept saying Ogino must hate me?"

"Hate her?" Ogino raised his voice, sounding truly shocked by this.

"I'm sorry. I shouldn't have brought it up . . ."

"No, I can't believe she thought I could hate her. Though I suppose I did hold it against her at the time. Right after she dumped me, I couldn't sleep properly for days. I was so sad. I wanted to see her. I just couldn't believe it. But I really loved your sister. She was the first person I truly fell in love with. I know we were

A Drop of Love

only high school students, but I really dreamed that we would be together for our whole lives. I mean, how would I ever meet someone more wonderful than her? Even though she'd dumped me, I still loved her from the bottom of my heart, and I couldn't believe that she was dead. No, I didn't want to believe it. The grief I'd felt when she dumped me was nothing compared to what I felt when she died."

I could hear the pain in his voice as he said this. His head hung down a little. It was like he was reliving the moment, like it happened yesterday and not six years ago. Then he seemed to come back to reality all of a sudden, and he looked over at me.

"Oh, I'm sorry. I'm going on and on about it. It's insensitive of me. I'm sure you don't want to hear about all that."

I shook my head without saying a word. Before I knew it, the beautiful garden and the ginkgo tree with its leaves stirring in the breeze had disappeared from view. All I saw was Ogino.

As I listened to him, my mind drifted back to the day my sister brought Ogino over.

My sister's name was Sumiré. She was born right after my parents started the Torunka.

Sumiré might sound like an old-fashioned name, but it fit my sister to a tee.

She was quiet and introverted. She liked reading and getting lost in her own thoughts.

Even at the café, she was always daydreaming in the corner with a paperback in her hand. She didn't stand out. She never drew attention to herself. In that way, she was maybe a little like our father.

Still, whenever I talked to her, she always listened. I loved my sister, the way she would nod along, saying very few words beyond "mhmmm, mhmmm" as she gave me her full attention. She wasn't an obvious beauty, yet there was something mysterious about her.

Whenever my sister was there, even just sitting in a seat in the corner of the Torunka, you could sense something different in the air. I wasn't the only one who could feel it, as evidenced by the fact that I often heard our regular customers talking about it too. "Oh," they'd say, "doesn't Sumiré look like she just popped out of a painting?"

So the Torunka Café's older daughter was mature and mysterious, and the younger daughter was spoiled and brimming with curiosity. That's how the adults in the neighborhood saw us.

A little after my sister started high school, she brought a somewhat older boy with her to the Torunka. A boy with a fair complexion and distinctly curly hair. He was very smart, but didn't look like he was very good at sports.

"This is Kazuhiko Ogino. He's my senpai at school," she said, looking a little embarrassed as she introduced him to us.

From then on, Ogino would stop by the café from time to time. At first, my sister called him Ogino Senpai. But before long, she switched to Kazu. Even though I was only in fifth grade, I could tell what that implied.

Ogino was gentle and easy to talk to. He was always kind to me and always smiling. But there was something about him that seemed out of sync with the world, like his feet were floating a few millimeters above the ground. Even as a child I could sense that peculiar quality about him. It was as if, deep down, behind his gentle smile, you could see that he'd already resigned himself. It was something I'd always secretly felt in my sister too.

The fact that they resembled each other in this way, and there was this resonance between them, was not something I could've put into words at the time. I was only vaguely aware of it, but this may have been what bound them together. That's how it seemed to me.

Because of that, I wasn't too fond of Ogino back then. The two of them were just too close; they seemed complete on their own. They didn't need anyone else, and so there was no room for me to be with them. When he was around, she seemed content in a way she never showed when she was with us. I could see a look of relief in her eyes that she'd finally found her anchor.

When he came over, I would suddenly find myself in a bad mood. He was stealing my sister.

Because I adored my sister, I was consumed by jealousy. It felt like a crisis. And I wasn't thrilled by the fact that my father and mother seemed completely smitten by him.

It was not long after my sister entered her second year of high school that he suddenly stopped showing up.

One day, I cautiously asked her, "What happened to Ogino?"

"I got tired of being with him," she said, as if it were nothing.

"You mean you broke up?"

"Yeah, I guess so."

I was stunned, yet I also knew that my sister was the kind of person who would quickly change her mind about things, so I couldn't say it was totally out of character. I guess that's how it goes, I thought, love's magic spell only lasts a short while. It doesn't go on forever. Taking this awfully philosophical view of the situation, I took the end of my sister's relationship as a kind of lesson. And I was secretly a little bit happy. Now, I thought, everything will go back to normal.

But that happiness didn't last. It wasn't long before my sister checked into the hospital.

I had no idea exactly what was going on. But the more time passed, the more I understood that the situation was becoming serious. When I learned there was no way to stop it, I discovered what true despair was. The so-called despair I'd felt that night I drank coffee was child's play. I couldn't believe that the world could be so sad and cruel. My sister got skinnier and skinnier until she became almost unrecognizable, and yet she still couldn't give up hope. Have you ever heard of anything so absurd?

My sister died at the end of August, three months after she checked into the hospital.

In the beginning, my sister, who was normally calm and composed, fell apart in a way that shocked me, and at times she would even take it out on my father and mother, but in the final month she became her normal self again, quiet and kind. She would welcome me to her room in the hospital, and happily listen as I told her about my day. Then she'd quietly smile. When she passed away her face still bore the traces of that smile. She looked as if she had drifted off to sleep.

At the funeral, I was in such a daze that I never shed a tear. My father and mother were out of it too. The three of us, the remaining members of the family, sat there stunned, like we were stuck in a dream. It was a humid day. I felt so tired that I was ready to fall down on the spot and give myself over to sleep.

Everything I saw was enveloped in a thin haze, and there, at the edge of my field of view, Ogino was crying. And trying to throw himself on the coffin.

What on earth is he crying about? I wondered.

A Drop of Love

I had no idea what had made him break down and sob like that.

That was the last time I'd seen Ogino until today.

By the time we left the museum, the sun was setting. It was now much cooler than the afternoon had been, and the deep blue color high up in the sky was growing darker.

As we said goodbye, I said once more with feeling, "So, please come back to the Torunka. Promise?" I wasn't really sure why, but I needed him to come to the café again.

"Okay, sure. Thank you," he said. "See you again. I'm glad we ran into each other."

He was just starting to head toward the station when I called after him, feeling that there was something I'd forgotten to say.

He turned back and looked at me curiously. "What is it?"

I was searching for the words to say, but nothing came to me.

"It's nothing. Thank you for the, um, iced tea."

He laughed. "I'll see you soon."

"Yes." I bowed to him as he waved goodbye, and then I started heading slowly in the opposite direction.

After my father and I had dinner together, just the two of us, I went out to pay Kōta a visit. I felt restless and heavyhearted, and I couldn't seem to shake the feeling. I just needed to talk to someone about what had happened that day. Plus, I knew if I told my father I was going to Kōta's house, he wouldn't ask any questions, even though I was going out at night.

It was a bright, moonlit night, and the temperature was milder than I expected. The hollyhocks blooming in my neighbor's garden were drooping after suffering through the afternoon heat. It felt good to walk down the deserted street in my sloppy outfit of sweatpants and a T-shirt. I shoved my hands in my pockets and walked briskly past the shuttered shops, all the while thinking of the day's events.

"See you soon," Ogino had said as he waved goodbye. I should've just casually waved back. Bowing was too formal.

But why did I find myself regretting something so trivial? These silly thoughts had me feeling surprisingly upset.

Outside Kōta's house, I rang the bell but only as a formality before I walked right in.

"Kōta, Shizu's here!"

"How many times do I have to tell you to call me Shizuku?" Yōhei somehow looked even more tan than this afternoon. I gave him my usual karate chop and said a quick hello to their mom on my way upstairs.

The instant I opened the door, I caught a faint whiff of a distinctive scent—I don't know if it's unique to Kōta, or if it's peculiar to all boys in puberty.

"Hey, babe, what can I do for you?"

Kōta, who was sitting in front of the TV screen with a video game controller in his hands, didn't even look at me when I came into the room. On the screen, a swarm of blood-drenched zombies was closing in on the guy Kōta was controlling.

He was still focused on smashing the buttons on the controller and hadn't looked up at me, so I poked him in the back with my toe, and said, "Don't you and your brother know how to act when a guest comes over?"

"You're not a guest."

A Drop of Love

He was always like that. But then again, maybe that's why he was easy to be around.

I looked around the room quickly, noticing the girl in the poster had changed since my last visit, but everything else was the same. I sat down on the bed, opened the bag of chips I found lying on the floor, and tossed a few into my mouth as I told him at length about the day's events, going on like I was talking to myself.

When I'd finished, Kōta didn't seem to show much interest. "Hmmm," he said, "Sumi's ex, huh? I've met him a bunch of times. Well, more like I passed him and Sumi on the street. He seemed quiet. Maybe that's why he and Sumi were a good match."

I'd expected more of a reaction—surprise or excitement maybe, but he seemed pretty indifferent. I was disappointed, even a little sad. When Kōta was little, he was very attached to my sister. There was a time when he was always chasing after her, calling, "Sumi, Sumi!" Though it didn't make any difference, his response still made me feel kind of lonely.

"So?"

"What do you mean 'so'?"

"What's the punch line?"

"There's no punch line. What are you talking about? I ran into him. That's all," I said, getting irritated. He really seemed to have no interest in the whole thing.

"Come on, normally when you tell a story like that, there's a punch line."

"What are you, some kind of Kansai comedian?"

"No sirree, Bob. I'm a Tokyo boy through and through."

I threw a pillow at him, but he dodged it nimbly without ever taking his eyes off the screen.

"Too slow, Joe."

He was so annoying. For some reason, his reflexes were ridiculously good. He was the only second year who managed to make it onto the regular squad of the volleyball club. And that's despite the fact he was always skipping practice. I'd heard that some third years were giving him a hard time about it, but he just shrugged it off with his trademark nonchalance. It's got to be pretty discouraging for them, dealing with a guy like that.

"But it's a good thing, right?" Kōta took his eyes from the screen for an instant and looked my way.

"What is?"

"You said he seems to be doing well. I mean if he was still holding on to all that, it would be pretty grim, right? It sounds like he's back on his feet again."

"Well, I guess so."

"Why do you sound so dissatisfied?"

"I'm not dissatisfied. It's definitely better that way."

"Oh."

Kōta was right. I agreed with him, of course.

But that wasn't what I wanted to tell him. I hadn't come all the way over here in the night just to tell him that Ogino was doing well. I wanted him to share my surprise that I'd run into him at all. When my sister died, I became painfully aware of how unfair the world can be. No one else outside my family could share in the pain I felt. But today, I felt as if Ogino had. And it made me feel both happy and sad. Behind those feelings, there was something else going on inside me. Yet there was no point in trying to tell all that to Kōta.

I couldn't put into words what I was feeling.

On the screen, the hero was surrounded by pale-faced zombies, cutting off his retreat. There was no way out. But Kōta didn't panic; he took aim at each zombie's head and disposed of them one by one. Each time he pressed the button on the controller, we heard the convincing bang of a gunshot and the flesh went flying.

"Hey, wait a second, isn't this game rated eighteen and over? What is this?"

I'd come because I wanted to shake off this heavyhearted feeling, but it hadn't gone away, and on top of that, he'd made me watch him play this gross game. I was getting more and more irritated. I'll give him something to pay attention to. I went behind his back and suddenly started tickling his belly. He'd been really ticklish ever since we were kids.

"Ahahaha, you idiot. I'm gonna die! Stop, seriously! Please!"

As expected, he lost control of the game, and the hero screamed in agony as he was brought down by the zombie horde. The black screen turned an awful blood red, and the words GAME OVER rose to the surface.

"What the heck are you doing? Can't you see that I'm all out of ammo now? My only option is to take my metal bat and go down swinging."

"What do I know? Maybe you're the one at fault for playing such an unhealthy game."

I started howling with laughter, remembering the funny look on Kōta's face when I was tickling him.

"What are you laughing at?"

Kōta threw a pillow at me, but I still couldn't stop laughing.

"I don't feel like playing anymore." He tossed the controller onto the floor and lay down.

"Hey, what's fun about going around killing zombies in that game?" I asked, genuinely curious.

"It's not like I particularly enjoy killing them. But we need to make sure the human race survives."

"Wouldn't it be better to coexist?"

"That's impossible. They're brain-dead. All they do is attack people blindly and increase their numbers. I mean, think about it.

"If our world was ever overrun with zombies, everyone would panic, you know? But not me. Because I've been preparing myself with the game. So you don't need to worry, Shizuku. If that day comes, you'll be the one I protect."

"Nope. Never happen."

"It might happen. If there's a viral outbreak."

What did he mean by viral outbreak? The game had completely warped his brain.

"Well, even if it does happen, I'd rather become a zombie than go on living in a world like that. I mean, most of the neighborhood would turn into zombies, right? My father, Chiyoko Bāchan, and Ayako, and Chinatsu and Shūichi . . ."

"In that case, I'll be a zombie too. We can be zombies together and build a happy little home." It didn't take much for Kōta to switch sides and join team Zombie.

"You think we could raise a family even if we're brain-dead?"

"Well, let's give up on the family idea, then, and just enjoy ourselves. We go through every day staggering around, living our lives. And occasionally we attack a human. We're serious about what we eat—we make sausages from their organs and smoke their arms and legs. That way we don't inflict too much pain on the people we eat. Might be nice to have a garden too. We could live the zombie version of the simple life." As Kōta said this, he started giggling like a little boy.

"Seriously, you are too big of an idiot for me to live with."

He really hadn't changed at all. I jumped up from the bed and headed for the door.

"Hey, Shizuku."

I turned back, startled. A second ago, he was lying on the ground, but now he was staring at me with a serious look on his face.

"What?" I asked warily.

"Are you okay?" he said in a softer voice.

"About what?"

"It's going to be the anniversary of the day Sumiré..."

"Oh..." When I finally understood what he meant, my voice grew quieter. Each year, near the end of August, as we approached the anniversary of my sister's death, my mind and my body would sort of break down. I'd get headaches and feel sick in my stomach, I'd feel terribly tense, the tiniest little thing could make me burst into tears. From the outside, you could tell my nerves were under strain all the time, and the things I said and the things I did got all mixed up somehow. The first year was especially awful. For a long time I couldn't get out of bed. That's what Kōta was talking about.

"I'm okay for now."

I checked the calendar on the wall. It was August 3. If it was going to happen again, I still had a little more time. "I mean, maybe things will be fine this year. It wasn't too bad last year, right?"

"I guess. I hope so. You're a little too fixated on Sumiré sometimes."

"What do you mean, I'm 'too fixated'?" I had no idea what he was talking about.

"Just what I said."

"I don't get it. She was my sister. Isn't that how it's supposed to be?"

"Yeah, but . . ." Kōta frowned and scratched the back of his head. "Well, nah, I don't know how to put it into words. Forget what I said. In any case, if you're ever having a hard time, just tell me, okay? You're not a complicated person. Nothing good's going to come from pretending everything's fine."

"Well, aren't you being awfully kind? Is this your plan to get me to forget about the five hundred yen I lent you the other day? I'm not that soft—I am the daughter of a former debt collector, after all," I said, fooling around. Kōta was being so earnest he didn't seem like himself at all. Hearing that sort of thing face-to-face was embarrassing.

"I'm worried about you is all. Is that a problem?" Kōta refused to take the bait. He was looking at me defiantly, probably trying to hide his own embarrassment.

I understood. Kōta was worried about me in his own peculiar way. Normally he acted like an idiot, but the truth was that no one was more concerned about me than he was. Although he could be a pain a lot of the time, I was grateful to have someone like him in my life. As I realized this, I found myself actually thanking him sincerely. "Hey, thanks for worrying about me. If anything happens, I'll let you know."

"Hmph."

Kōta turned away from me until I left the room.

It was close to a week later that Ogino stopped by the Torunka. It was already getting close to the Obon festival.

I hadn't gone out at all that week despite the fact that it was my summer vacation. Instead, I'd been helping out at the café from morning to night, filling in for Shūichi.

But I was well aware that that wasn't the only reason. In some corner of my mind, I was waiting for Ogino to arrive.

Ogino stood for a moment in the doorway, lit up in his sky-blue shirt by the fierce sunlight from outside, and looked around the café. Behind his glasses, his eyes narrowed with nostalgia. Then he smiled slightly, as though he was relieved to see that nothing at all had changed.

"Welcome."

The moment he walked in my heart leapt in my chest, but I didn't dare let it show. I welcomed him with a little smile.

"Oh, Shizuku. I hope you don't mind that I took you up on your offer."

Once my father saw Ogino, he instantly smiled and called him over to the counter. "I was wondering if that was you. It must be hot outside. Come sit here."

"Sir, I'm sorry it's been so long."

It was funny—Ogino had seemed so mature until that moment, but the way he said those words made him sound like a kid afraid of being scolded.

"I heard you and Shizuku happened to run into each other. I'm glad you came. And that you've grown into such a fine young man," my father said as he stared at Ogino, his voice making clear how deeply happy he was. It was pretty rare to see my father smile from ear to ear like that.

One of our regulars, Old Mr. Takita, who was watching their conversation, whispered, "Who's that, Shizuku?"

"He was a friend of my sister's."

"Oh, a friend of Sumiré's."

Old Mr. Takita's eyes lit up. He was always eager to poke his nose into whatever was going on. Well, leave him be, I thought. He's weird like that.

"Um, sir," Ogino said timidly.

My father gave him a curious look. "What is it?"

Old Mr. Takita and I were side by side at the far end of the counter, eavesdropping.

"I'm truly sorry about what happened at Sumiré's funeral. My behavior was inexcusable."

"What are you talking about? There's absolutely no reason to get worked up about that now. Is that what kept you from coming to the café?" My father stared at him in disbelief. Then he turned to me and said, "Sheesh, Shizuku, say something to him."

"I already told him," I said.

Ogino scratched the back of his head in embarrassment.

"Then there's nothing more for me to say. It would be ridiculous for us to lose touch over something like that."

"I apologize."

"Did you leave town for college?"

"Yes, but I found a job here, so I'm back in the city again."

"Your parents must be happy."

"Not exactly. I ended up finding a job at a start-up. My mother would have preferred a bigger, more stable company. She's still giving me grief about it. But I prefer the feeling of working at a smaller company where my work really matters. Oh, here's my card." Ogino held out his business card, and my father happily accepted it.

"Really? I'm sure you'll thrive in any job," he said, giving Ogino his seal of approval. My father was normally so stern with everyone that Old Mr. Takita sat there watching him, his eyes wide with surprise.

Still in a good mood, my father prepared the cup of Guatemalan coffee that Ogino had ordered. Using the electric mill, he ground the freshly roasted beans that had arrived from the roasting plant earlier in the day, put the kettle on the range, placed the grounds in the filter, and carefully poured boiling water over them. Ogino watched my father work in silence, fascinated. As I watched the two of them, I thought about how many times I'd seen this scene before.

The porcelain cup gleamed. As it was filled to the brim with black liquid, the aroma filled the whole room. Though I detest coffee, I still love that aroma. It's strange the way those grounds can give off such a soothing aroma when they're transformed into coffee.

"Sorry to keep you waiting."

When my father placed the cup of coffee in front of him, Ogino said thank you and raised the cup to his lips.

"It's as good as I remember," he said with a satisfied smile, placing the cup in the saucer. Just seeing him smile like that, I knew that I hadn't pressured him to come back to the café in vain.

"You don't think the flavor's lost anything?"

"No, not at all. It's just right. I've been waiting for this. It makes me so happy to taste it again after all this time. I'm glad I came today. Actually, before I came here today, I stopped by Sumiré's grave."

"Is that right? Thank you. I'm sure Sumiré was happy. So please, don't hold back. Come whenever you like."

"I will."

When I saw the cheerful look on Ogino's face, my heart leapt in my chest again.

"Hmmm, he seems like a pretty nice young man. Reminds me of myself in my younger days," Old Mr. Takita whispered in my ear.

"He is," I agreed, pretending I hadn't heard the second part.

Then, after a moment, Ogino got up from his seat. *Just stay a little longer*, I said to myself. My father stopped him, but he said he had plans to meet someone for work.

"I'll come back."

"You're welcome anytime."

What could I do? I was secretly panicking. Ogino was leaving. Though I had no idea why I felt this way, I knew I didn't want him to go. I tried to think of a reason to keep him there. But before I could think of one, he had finished paying his bill.

"See you later, Shizuku," he said and reached for the door.

"Um, I need to pick up some things for dinner."

It might have been a bit of a lame excuse. I'd just gone food shopping the day before, and on top of that, I'd said I was buying extra to stock up because I didn't want to go out today. I could feel the embarrassment welling up inside me as I glanced at my father. But he didn't seem to mind at all. He just replied in his usual brusque way, "Oh yeah, thanks."

I felt a wave of relief.

"In that case, I'll walk you there," Ogino said with a smile. But just like before, it was the way you'd smile when you were talking to a child.

It was the time of day when the setting sun shines directly on the market street, and as soon as we started walking, I was covered

A Drop of Love

in sweat. Having taken off my apron, I was only wearing a loose white top and short shorts, which made me feel even more like a child, walking alongside Ogino, who looked so mature. Still, the clothes in my dresser were all more or less the same, so whatever I'd chosen to wear today wouldn't have made much of a difference.

"Hot out today, isn't it?" Ogino said, wiping the sweat from his forehead.

"It is. Doesn't it seem like on TV they say every year that it's an unusually hot summer? It's like, when are we going to get a normal summer?"

"Hahaha, you're absolutely right."

"You know? My father says summer is supposed to be hot, but I think there's more to it than that."

It got to the point where I was lying, and yet our silly little conversation kept going. I no longer had an idea what I was trying to do, but I kept on talking, afraid of letting a moment of silence come between us.

"So how was coming back to the Torunka after so long?"

"Really nostalgic. It was a relief to see that nothing had changed. The atmosphere and the taste of your father's coffee were exactly the same. You had that poster of *A Midsummer Night's Dream* on the wall back then too, right? I can't believe it's still there."

"We got that from the movie theater and hung it up because my mother loves it. It's been up there for I don't know how many years."

Ogino was talking about the poster of the famous Czech artist and puppet animator Jiří Trnka. Trnka passed away a long time ago, and his film of Shakespeare's *A Midsummer Night's Dream* was made more than fifty years ago, but it's so delicate and beautiful that you'd never believe it was that old. Watching it, you felt like you were being drawn into a world of kaleidoscopic colors. Because of my mother, I've seen the film on DVD many times since I was a child. When I was little, I couldn't understand the story, but I was struck by how beautiful it was. When it was over, I always had tears in my eyes.

"And am I right that the café is named after the director?"

"Yes. Apparently my mother and father went on their first date to see a special screening of Trnka's film at a little art-house theater. Later on, when they decided to take over the café, my mother had a feeling they should name it after Jiří Trnka. She was like, 'What if we write out his name in Japanese? We could call our place the Torunka Café.'"

"Wow, I never knew that. That's great. The café's name comes from one of their memories."

"Well, from what they told me, they mostly just liked the way it sounded. If Jiří Trnka ever found out, as he lay there in his grave, that there was a little café named after him in Japan he'd probably be quite surprised. I hope he doesn't mind that we made his name a little easier to say in Japanese."

Ogino chuckled when I said this, and then looked up at the sky, which was changing color as the sun set.

"That reminds me. Sumiré liked that movie too. The first day I ever went to the café, I asked what movie the poster was for, and she laughed at me and said, 'You don't know Jiří Trnka?' So, I rushed out to buy the DVD."

"She said that to you?" I said, surprised. "That's pretty cruel. I mean, my sister only knew about him because of our mother."

But for some reason Ogino seemed happy. Then, right as we walked past the produce market, I realized something—I'd for-

A Drop of Love

gotten my wallet. A battalion of middle-aged women, who were probably tourists, were coming toward us. Ogino and I quickly stepped aside to get out of their way.

"We were a bit competitive like that when it came to what each of us knew," Ogino said. "We were just a couple of kids with overactive egos. But even at that age, Sumiré knew all kinds of things, probably because she'd read a ton of books."

"That's true," I said. My sister knew so much that I was always scratching my head, wondering where she'd learned it all.

"You know the story behind why bookmarks are called shiori? Apparently, the term comes from the way people walking through the mountains would break branches along the way to mark their path. Over time, the meaning shifted, so that the word 'shiori' came to mean the thing you leave in a book to mark your page. That's why the original characters were written 枝折り *shiori*, which literally means breaking a branch. Sumiré once told me that quite proudly, adding, 'Of course, you knew that already, didn't you, Ogino Senpai?' Even now, whenever I leave a bookmark in a book, I remember the look on her face."

"We didn't really get to see that side of her," I said quietly, as I tried to imagine the expression on her face then. "Though she did have a bit of a high opinion of herself at times."

"We used to get into little fights over it. In the end, I was always the one to give in."

I guess my sister may have depended on Ogino in a way. Maybe it was because I was much younger, or because of her innate pride, but she really didn't lean on us like that. Ogino, in that sense, must have been very special to her. It was because of him that she was able to show off how much she knew and get into those little arguments, always knowing that he would be the one to give in.

I was still lost in those thoughts when we came to the end of the market street.

"You were going food shopping, right?"

By the time Ogino asked this, he already had one foot on the steps of the Sunset Stairs. To hold him there a little longer, I said the first thing that came to mind: "What should I get for dinner tonight?"

It seemed to do the trick. Ogino stepped down from the stairs and turned around. "That reminds me, your father was telling me that your mother is in another country now? I guess that's why you're taking care of things at home. That's impressive," he said with genuine admiration.

Flustered, I said, "It's my job for the time being. My mother's in Chiang Mai," I said quickly, going into more detail than necessary.

"Wow, Chiang Mai, that's deep in the mountains in Thailand, right?" he asked, turning to face me fully.

At the edge of the steps, a trio of cats were sitting in a row, watching us drowsily.

"When my sister died, things got sort of overwhelming. It's like we didn't have the space to feel anything else," I said, struggling to find the words to explain myself. I'd just meant to keep him from leaving, but now I was kicking myself. It was a hard thing to explain. If I said too much, I'd end up being pitied, but if I said too little, it could lead to a misunderstanding. The right thing to do, normally, was to say nothing. So I'd failed again. But Ogino, it seemed, understood me well enough. He nodded and listened to me. That was all. I was relieved to see there was no sign of pity in his face.

"So then, my mom and dad talked things over with a counselor, and he suggested that we try changing things at home for the time being. That led to my mother going over to join a non-profit in Thailand about three years ago. They're helping villages rebuild. They dig wells and work in the fields. I'm not exactly sure where they are now. They go from one village to the next."

"Is that right? From one to the next?" Ogino paused then like he was trying to find the words to say something. "It must've been hard," he said. And those few words were enough to convey his compassion. It made my heart feel less heavy.

"My mom has been doing much better recently because of that decision. She's having a good time. When she was a student, she used to volunteer in organizations like that," I said cheerfully. "It might not look like it but I don't hate housework. I guess maybe being a housewife suits me."

That might be true, actually. Things were working out well at home for us now, because we'd found a balance. If we'd tried to keep going as a normal family, the whole thing would probably have fallen apart a long time ago. Of course, there were times when I was sad that my mother wasn't there, but I knew I could handle it. Even if we were apart, it didn't mean we stopped being a family.

"Shizuku." Ogino called my name. His face was lit up by the colors of the sunset. "You really are remarkable. I admire you. Some people, like me, become adults merely by growing older, without doing anything in particular. You're much more of an adult than I am."

I didn't need a mirror to show me that even my ears were blushing.

"No, no, please. I'm just a kid. My old friend tells me that all the time. He says, 'You think like a kid. Everything is simple to you.' And he's totally right. I just don't want anyone to get hurt. I want everyone to be happy. My family, all the people I know, and all the customers at the café."

I hated how childish I sounded. And I had no doubt that that's exactly how I sounded to Ogino.

"I'm sure I come off as incredibly arrogant and infantile. And not just arrogant, but hypocritical. I sometimes get fed up with my own self-righteousness."

Ogino slowly shook his head and looked straight at me.

"You're a girl who cares about people. What you're talking about isn't arrogant or hypocritical. It's kind. You're able to see things that way because you've experienced true sadness."

I looked down, flustered. Ogino had been staring back at me, and I couldn't meet his eyes. My whole body was covered in sweat, and it probably wasn't just from the heat. For some reason, I felt like I might cry. I kept my eyes on the road, unable to look back at Ogino's face.

"I'm sorry. I've held you up for too long. I should go too," I said, feeling like if we spent any more time together I would say something even more foolish.

"You're right. I'll see you soon, okay?"

I hurried back toward the market street without waiting for Ogino to say any more. As I walked, I was greeted by all the people I knew, but I could offer only the most perfunctory responses.

Oh, is that what this is? I get it now. That's what's happening, I said to myself as I passed through the busy market.

Ever since I ran into Ogino, I'd felt restless and heavyhearted, unable to understand why I felt that way.

But I finally realized the source of that feeling.

I might actually be in love.

I might be in love with Ogino.

Yikes. I was having trouble believing it myself.

I ran home, feeling like screaming at the top of my lungs.

The moment I realized this, I knew I was in trouble. With each passing day, the truth became more and more irrefutable, overwhelming my defenses.

Before I knew it, Ogino was all I could think of, day and night. All I could do was dream of the next time I would see him.

It was hard to make sense of it. When on earth had I started feeling this way about him? I'd fallen in love with him just from seeing him twice, after being reunited with him after six years. And it's not like we said very much to each other.

But I suppose maybe love is like that. A few innocent words, a brief encounter can mean so much. I guess that's how it works. After all, people even fall in love at first sight.

That day, as we walked from the café, I said things to Ogino that I'd never shared with anyone before. He didn't laugh at me; he listened, and he understood what I was feeling. And that was enough to save me. Nothing like that had ever happened to me before. I felt so happy I could cry.

Yes, Ogino understood me. And my trust in him was probably what led me to fall unexpectedly in love. At least, that's how it seemed to me at that moment. The heaviness I'd been feeling had suddenly lifted.

Love is incredible, isn't it? I could understand a little bit better now why Chinatsu always had that look on her face. Unless you've been in love, you'll never know that intensity of emotion.

And yet having said that, just realizing what I was feeling wasn't going to change the situation, even if I was walking around mooning over Ogino.

From that point on, Ogino came by the café every few days. He'd show up at night on his way home from work, or wander in around lunchtime on his day off. In the space of a week, he managed to come three times. Yet I barely talked to him. I said hello, and made a little small talk—that's all.

What mattered to Ogino was the ambience of the café and my father's coffee. I was just a part of the package.

If I'd felt like I was the complimentary dessert you got when you bought something at the convenience store, I might not have minded so much. But in my case, I mattered less than the bonus footage they throw in with a DVD. From Ogino's body language, I could tell that he saw me as nothing more than his little sister. It was obvious whenever we came into contact.

"Hey, Shizuku, you're helping out at the café again? I'm impressed. You don't want to go to the pool?"

It pained me to hear him say this in a sweet little voice. Hadn't he told me that I was an adult, not long ago? I wasn't acting any differently. It was becoming quite clear to me that the real problem was that I was less appealing than my sister.

From the time we were little, my sister was the one who tended to stand out more, so I grew up without much confidence in that department. Until now, I'd been fine keeping love at a distance, but now I was suffering for it.

I couldn't quit now though. After all, this was the first time I'd ever been in love.

Still, I wasn't going to get any further like this. How on earth could I get Ogino to take a real look at me?

Should I wear skimpy clothes? Nope, that was out of the question. I'm not sexy at all, so if I dressed like that I'd just look even more childish. Besides, Ogino didn't seem like the kind of guy who was attracted to that sort of thing.

Maybe I could change the way I talked. Like, what if I tried to sound cute and girly? Nope, out of the question, again. Just imagining myself talking like that made me want to throw up.

As I lay there on my bed, staring up at the ceiling, laying out one strategy after another, a thought occurred to me. It was an unbelievably simple and straightforward idea. Why hadn't I thought of it before?

I leapt from bed in the middle of the night and tiptoed out of my room. Then I opened the door to the room next to mine and turned on the light.

The room had remained largely untouched since my sister left it. The desk where she studied, the bookshelves and curtains, were exactly the same. The little bird mobile that I had given her for her last birthday was still dangling from the ceiling. Aside from the dustiness, you could be forgiven for thinking my sister was actually still living there. Here alone time had stopped on the day my sister was brought to the hospital.

Neither my father nor my mother nor I ever considered cleaning out the room. All we did was occasionally air out the futon and vacuum in order to keep things the same.

As I stood there in the middle of the room staring blankly, I heard my father call me from the hallway.

"What are you doing in there, Shizuku?"

"Do you think I could borrow some of Sumiré's clothes?"

My father had a strange expression on his face for a moment, then he mumbled, "Sure, I don't see any problem with that. But haven't you always said that you didn't want to wear her clothes because they weren't your style?"

"I changed my mind."

"Did something happen?"

"I just feel differently now."

My father shrugged and said, "Be careful with them," then walked away.

The moment I opened the closet, I was hit by the smell of camphor. I picked out a few summer outfits—a white lace dress, a chic purple dress, and a bright yellow dress. They were all dresses. In summer, dresses were my sister's staple. After holding up each one and studying it, I decided that the bright yellow dress was the one that seemed most summery and would look best on me.

My sister died at seventeen. Now I was seventeen. Based on our ages at least, this was the closest we were going to get.

I stared at my reflection in the full-length mirror, wearing my sister's dress. I felt like something was off. It was my hair. I undid my ponytail and tried brushing my hair out with my fingers. But my soft, fine hair didn't fall neatly to my shoulders like my sister's, it instantly curled at the ends.

I looked at myself in the mirror and whispered, "Oh, Ogino, don't you know Jiří Trnka?" but I was hit by a wave of embarrassment. Still, I was starting to think that the dress itself looked pretty good on me, or at least, not as bad as I'd imagined.

All right. I looked at my reflection in the mirror and nodded.

After our time off for Obon, I immediately put on that yellow dress and showed up for work. I was wearing my work apron over the dress and had my hair down as usual, at shoulder length. I was also wearing my sister's black high heels.

"Why, don't you look awfully pretty today, Shizuku," Chiyoko Bāchan said to me when she came in first thing in the morning.

"Really?" Her reaction had put me in a very good mood. "These are my sister's actually."

"Oh, Sumiré's. You've grown up, Shizuku. And to think it wasn't long ago that you were just a baby," she said, sounding very moved. Her eyes narrowed as she looked off into the distance.

"Baby" was definitely taking it a bit far, but I was genuinely happy that someone had recognized that I'd changed.

After I chuckled a little out of embarrassment, I decided to double-check her response. "It doesn't look weird on me?"

"It's quite flattering. You look very feminine and pretty."

And later on, when Shūichi came in that afternoon for his first shift in a while, he seemed pretty astonished.

"That was a surprise. I come back after a bit and there's a girl here I don't recognize."

He seemed to be in an unusually good mood, probably because he'd celebrated his birthday the day before. He was already using the bag Chinatsu had gotten him as a present.

"You don't think I look weird at all, Sylvie?"

"What do you mean, 'Sylvie'? Really though, I think it looks good on you. I'm sure Kōta will fall in love with you all over again."

As for my father, his response was curt: "Well, maybe it's not so bad after all." He didn't even try to look me in the eye. But I let it go, figuring that he probably had complex feelings about seeing me in Sumiré's clothes.

Unfortunately, Ogino didn't show up that day. Still, the approval from everyone at the Torunka had boosted my confidence, so from then on, I started wearing a new outfit of my sister's every day. In the beginning, I felt uncomfortable, like I was wearing clothes that were the wrong size, but little by little that feeling faded. Instead, as I put on my sister's clothes, I felt like I was actually becoming my sister. It felt surprisingly good, and it lifted my spirits.

I got carried away then, and rather than being satisfied with just her clothes, I started wearing hair clips and brooches that I borrowed from my sister's wardrobe. I consulted pictures I pulled from the photo album, to see how to coordinate my outfits. I tried imitating her gestures and the way she walked based on what I remembered.

I started to wonder if maybe I was taking it a little too far. I'd lost sight of my original goal. The thought occurred to me when I caught sight of my reflection in the window of the café and I suddenly came to my senses, but I didn't stop myself. I didn't even try.

Then, one day, Ogino finally came by.

Ogino walked in and went straight to the counter and sat down, without even noticing my existence. When I quietly approached him, he seemed shocked.

"What? You surprised me. Is that you, Shizuku? Why are you dressed like that?"

"Is something wrong?" I asked in reply, my heart pounding in my chest.

"No, nothing's wrong, but you seem so different. And"—Ogino mumbled as he looked me up and down—"those clothes are Sumiré's, right?"

"You can tell? I decided it was time for a bold new look," I said as I casually brushed my hair back so he could notice my hair clip.

"Really? Oh, I guess that's good, then."

Ogino's reaction wasn't quite what I was hoping for, but at least he was clearly looking at me differently. That was enough for me to be rather satisfied. At any rate, I needed him to take an interest in me before I could make him fall in love with me.

All right, let's do this. In my mind, I gave myself a little fist pump.

At first, things went according to plan: when Ogino was heading home, I left, under the same pretense as last time, that I had to go shopping. Now that I had turned into my sister, I was feeling surprisingly bold. As we left the café, I didn't get flustered the way I did last time. At this rate, I might end up getting carried away and confessing my love for him. Okay, let's do it, I said to myself as we left Torunka Street and joined the market street.

But right then, I suddenly felt someone grab my arm and pull me back.

When I turned around in surprise, I saw Kōta glaring at me with a sullen look on his face I'd never seen before.

"Hey, what the hell?" Wincing, I managed to pull the arm Kōta was squeezing free from his powerful grip.

"What are you doing?" Kōta said, still glaring at me.

"That ought to be my line. What's got into you?"

Ogino's mouth was hanging open as he looked back and forth at Kōta and me. Kōta turned and quickly bowed. "Oh, hello."

"Oh, nice to see you. Are you, um, Shizuku's friend?"

"I don't know this guy" is what I felt like saying, but instead, I reluctantly said, "Yes."

"Pardon. We, uh, have some business to attend to." Kōta smiled cheerfully at Ogino, hiding the look of open hostility he'd been showing me.

"Oh, is that right? Well, I'll be on my way, then."

He seemed easily persuaded. For Ogino, none of this was especially interesting, I guess. "See you, Shizuku," he said and walked away briskly down the market street.

As soon as I was sure that Ogino was gone, I went after Kōta. "What the hell! You idiot!"

"What're you doing?" Kōta said, not seeming especially bothered.

"What? Like I told you, I should be the one saying that."

I was getting agitated, and now I was shouting, which drew the attention of some middle-aged women out shopping. Kōta grabbed my arm again and pulled me back into the alley.

For a moment the two of us glared at each other in the dim light of the alley. Once he started his second year of middle school, he hit a growth spurt, and before you knew it, he was much taller than me. It had already gotten to the point where I couldn't make eye contact with him if I didn't make an effort and look up. In the past, I could dominate him, not only in our arguments, but also in physical strength, but now I was no match for him.

"Wait, do you have a crush on that guy?"

I could feel embarrassment and outrage flaring up inside me. Where did Kōta get off asking me a question like that? What was wrong with him? Not only did he stop me from spending time with Ogino, now he had to go and make it worse by asking that? And I didn't appreciate him threatening me either.

"It's got nothing to do with you!" I shouted, trying to outshout Kōta.

"Are you an idiot? He's Sumiré's boyfriend," he said, sounding irritated.

A Drop of Love

"Not anymore."

Kōta didn't say anything for a moment, then he took a deep breath and let it out. He'd told me before that it was something his coach taught him to do when things got intense in a volleyball match.

"I'm sorry I accosted you out of nowhere. I'm sure it was rude to Ogino too. I apologize."

"It's fine," I said, regaining my composure a little. "Anyway, Ogino didn't seem to mind."

"Well, it was wrong of me. But let me ask you something. What do you like about him? How well do you even know him?"

When Kōta asked the question, I found myself unexpectedly unable to reply. What was it that I liked about Ogino? Ever since I realized that I was in love with him, I'd been so busy thinking about that fact and wondering how I could get his attention, that I hadn't really considered why I felt that way. Ogino was kind. And gentle. That's about all I knew. Aside from the fact that he had been my sister's boyfriend, I didn't really know much about Ogino as a person...

"If you're going to put me on the spot like that, I don't really know what to say. But I love him."

"Really?" Kōta studied my face earnestly.

I nodded, feeling the urge to avert my eyes.

Then he looked me up and down and said, "Well then, go for it, but be your normal self."

"What do you mean?"

"Don't dress like that. I'm saying go for it, if that's what you want, but be Shizuku, not someone else. I mean, what are you doing dressed like that? It doesn't look good on you at all."

To be honest, it hurt to hear that. But it didn't really matter what Kōta thought about what I wore.

"It's none of your business. I've put a lot of thought into it. I mean, if Ogino isn't interested in me the way I normally am, then..." My voice got quieter.

"So, you're fine if he falls for you dressed up as Sumiré?"

I couldn't argue with Kōta's quick retort. I could feel my blood boiling again. But Kōta just went right on talking.

"It's like I was saying before. You're too fixated on your sister. After I saw how you reacted to seeing Ogino again, I was worried that something strange was going to happen. If you truly are in love with Ogino, then I'm fine with that. If that's the case, then I'll even support you. But do it fair and square, don't go running back to Sumiré."

"Shut up!" I realized I was screaming. The sound of my voice reverberated in the narrow street and made Kōta's eyes go wide.

"What are you angry about? I'm saying this for your own good. Didn't I tell you I was worried about you? Why can't you underst—"

"Shut up! Shut up! I told you it was none of your business. Now, get out of here!"

I didn't understand why I was so angry at Kōta. But I couldn't stop myself. Kōta's brow twitched for an instant, and then immediately furrowed.

"What the hell. I'm the one talking calmly here. Fine. I get it. I won't worry about you anymore."

"I don't need your concern."

"Okay, I get it. I get it. Whatever. I don't care what happens to you. Don't talk to me ever again."

After tossing off that last line, Kōta abruptly spun around and

A Drop of Love

walked off into the bright light of the market street. Even when I yelled, "That goes for you too!" he didn't bother to look back.

"Ah, why does beer taste so good when you drink it outside?" Ayako said after taking a big gulp. She was already on her third pint. Ayako was normally a pretty cheerful person, but with a little alcohol in her, she became twice as lively. But no matter how much she drank, it never showed in her face.

It was our yearly tradition: the Yanaka Ginza festival. The market street was completely transformed with brightly colored stands lining the street. The festival was packed with events—starting with a fish-catching event for kids in the afternoon, there were band performances, Obon dances, and wild processions of men carrying shrines through the streets.

Ayako had her sights set on the draft beer fair that started in the evening (and was basically an event with cheap beer). For the past few years, for some reason, she'd always taken me with her to the event. "It's no fun to drink alone," she'd told me, but before I knew it she was hitting it off with some men who were similarly drunk. For some time now, they'd been raising their glasses and exchanging toasts.

Even though this was a once-a-year festival, I was in a dark mood. With a now lukewarm coke in my hand from the draft beer fair tent, I looked out at the people dressed in yukata crowding the street.

I was still dealing with the aftermath of what happened with Kōta. Why had it felt so tense? We'd had more fights up to this point than there were stars in the sky, but this one felt fundamentally different. How can I describe it? It was a real fight. But

Kōta was out of line. He was butting in though it had nothing to do with him. And the way he talked to me was incredibly insensitive. Like he could ever understand what it was like to be a girl in love.

And yet something he'd said was still lodged in my heart.

So, you're fine if he falls for you dressed up as Sumiré?

That would be okay, I thought. I believed that was the right answer. But Kōta had said I should be myself if I was going to go for it. The thought hadn't occurred to me until he said that. Maybe I was getting a little weird. August 28, the anniversary of my sister's death, would be here in four days. It's possible that, without my realizing it, the anniversary was making me act strangely. Maybe I had gone a little bit crazy without realizing it. As I thought about it, I felt a chill run down my back.

You're too fixated on your sister.

Kōta had said that too. But what could that possibly mean? She was my sister, what was wrong with being fixated on her? It was hard to hear that from Kōta, who acted like he'd totally forgotten about her and didn't care anymore. As those thoughts went around and around in my head, I heard, mixed in with the traditional festival music, the sound of Yōhei's voice. "Hey Kōta, it's Shizuku. And Ayako's there too."

He was coming this way, with his little shaved head bobbing up and down and a double serving of grilled corn and candied apple in his hands.

I froze when I saw who was beside him. Kōta. What should I do? Should I say something? But Kōta walked right by with a blank look on his face, even though I was sure our eyes met, and he must've caught a glimpse of me panicking.

He acted like we were total strangers. Yōhei was tugging at

A Drop of Love

the sleeve of his T-shirt, but he didn't turn to look. He just disappeared into the crowd.

Over the speakers, I could hear the announcement calling out to us in vain, "The Obon Dance will be starting shortly. We invite you all to join in."

"Are you two fighting?" Ayako gave me a quizzical look as she downed her fourth beer.

"Yeah, well..."

I took a gulp of my warm coke, trying to hide my trembling hands.

"Aha," Ayako said, teasing. "So that's why you've had that hangdog look on your face. If it's bad enough to make you look that sad, you ought to make up with him."

"I...I don't feel like making up."

"Tsk, tsk, I guess you're only young once." She laughed until her slender shoulders shook. Just as I was telling myself she was already drunk and I should leave her there and go home, she asked abruptly, "By the way, Shizuku, what's up with you dressing like Sumiré?" Until that point, she'd shown no sign of noticing.

"It doesn't look good on me?"

"To put it plainly, no. It doesn't."

"No way. Everyone at the Torunka told me I looked nice."

It came as a pretty big shock to hear that—first from Kōta, then from Ayako, of all people.

"Listen, it's not that bad. You look cute in a way that's much more girlish. But I like you better the way you are."

"Really?"

"And is that the reason you and Kōta are fighting?"

From time to time, she could be so clever that it was genuinely scary. She could even pull it off when she was drunk. I clenched the empty cup in my hand and hung my head.

"Yeah. Kōta was lecturing me, and I got really angry. I mean, he was talking about things he didn't understand, and he was being scary, and he wasn't acting like himself."

"Hey, Shizuku," she said, gently admonishing me. You know the quote 'Better keep yourself clean and bright. You are the window through which you must see the world.' It's from an English playwright."

"What does it mean?"

I gave her a puzzled look, the way I always did with her mysterious quotations.

"Hmmm? You don't get it? Basically, the world is all mixed up, the good and the bad, the wheat and the chaff. You've got things that are naturally beautiful and things that are fake. What you choose to believe in is up to you. So the important thing is to become a sensible person, you know, polish yourself, keep yourself clean and bright. And vice versa. The world sees you too. So that's another reason why it's important to work on yourself, to polish yourself. At least, that's how I interpret the quote."

It sounded a little bit like the story behind my name. My father had named me Shizuku, which means "a drop," because he hoped that my life would be as rich and flavorful as a drop of good coffee.

"I, I mean I've been trying to work on myself, but . . ." What was wrong with what I'd been doing? I couldn't tell anymore. I was confused.

"I know. I get it. But I think maybe there's something off about the way you've been polishing yourself. It's hard to watch you go through this. It's like you're forcing it. You have to try to work on

A Drop of Love

what makes you you. There's a lot of people who come to the Torunka just to see your smile. That smile can be enough to help them through their day. I'm sure that's what Kōta meant to say. It's just that he's an idiot and he did a terrible job explaining himself."

"Maybe you're right," I said, though I didn't know how to start working on what made me me. Was that really what Kōta was trying to say? I didn't know. But I felt like I understood now that he was trying to look out for me. Because he was the person who was closest to me and knew me best, he'd volunteered to play that thankless role. Or maybe he didn't even think it through that carefully. But either way, I was the one at fault.

"I know that at your age there's a lot of uncertainty. And on top of all that, you've got everything with Sumiré. I'm sure there's a lot on your mind. But you don't need to rush things. Working on yourself takes an incredible amount of time." Ayako stopped then and added, "But listen to me, going on and pretending to be so wise. I'm not in a position to be giving lectures, so I'll stop here. Thanks for hearing me out." Then she gave me an encouraging pat on the shoulder.

"Time for another beeeer!" she announced, like she was singing a line from a song. She headed in the direction of the beer stand, charging into the street where the Obon Dance had just begun.

I was standing in front of the gates to Nippori Station, waiting for Ogino.

It was nearly eight o'clock. In the deep darkness of the summer night, only the entrance of the station was brightly lit. The swarm of insects that had been attracted to the lights were now circling the fluorescent bulbs.

The night of the festival, I had been up worrying till dawn, and I came to the conclusion that I would tell Ogino how I felt. I called him the next evening and asked him if he'd meet me. He said he was about to leave work and would meet me here.

I had been thinking over things ever since my talk with Kōta. I probably thought about the situation more than I'd ever thought about anything before. And in the end, I decided that I should be myself. I wouldn't wear my sister's clothes. I would be me, and I would tell Ogino exactly how I felt. If I'd talked it over with a friend, they probably would've tried to stop me. "It's too soon," they'd say. "You've got to get to know each other first." But once I made my decision, it was full speed ahead. That's just how I am. I had to be true to what I was feeling for him in that moment. I didn't want to play games or strategize. Even if it went badly, I wouldn't have any regrets as long as it was what I'd decided.

And when it was all settled, I'd go apologize to Kōta. I didn't know if he'd forgive me, but even if he didn't, I'd just apologize some more. If he didn't forgive me the first day, then I'd try again the next day. And I'd go on apologizing no matter how many years it took, until Kōta gave in and said, "Okay, I get it. Fine."

I thought about all this as I carefully watched the gates of the station, feeling restless. Time seemed to move unbelievably slowly. I was sure that a half hour had gone by, but when I checked the clock in the station, it had been only five minutes.

I watched as another train arrived and departed the station. It was the fifth one since I arrived. After a moment, a crowd of people came pouring through the gates.

A Drop of Love

"Ah." When my eyes came to rest on one man in particular, dressed in a suit, the sound escaped my lips.

At the same moment, he turned to me, and his face broke into a smile. Now he was coming my way, still smiling. That was enough to make my heart beat faster. He'd found me. And that was enough to make me happy.

"Sorry to keep you waiting," Ogino said, checking his watch once he was standing right there in front of me.

"No, I'm the one who called you out of the blue and asked you to come."

He gave a quick bow. "It's already pretty late. Are you sure it's okay?"

"It's fine."

Then Ogino noticed my outfit: a pale blue T-shirt and faded jeans.

"Oh, you're back to your regular style." He grinned.

"Yeah, tonight I'm just my regular self." I smiled.

We walked together into the cemetery, surrounded by dense greenery. The moonlight shone through the gaps in the trees. The other people who had left the station after Ogino now passed us as we walked together. The piercing sound of cicadas had ceased entirely, and in its place we could hear the clear *reeeen reeen* sound of other insects somewhere in the night.

"So what was it you wanted to talk to me about? Are you looking for advice about something?"

Ogino seemed to have no idea what I was about to tell him. Well, from his point of view that was only natural. I was the one who was nervous to be standing beside him at last.

"Is something wrong?" Ogino gave me a puzzled look.

"Um..."

"What is it?"

But the words I'd rehearsed so many times in my head somehow wouldn't come out. If I kept on acting nervous and out of sorts, we'd be at the market street in no time. I closed my eyes tight and took a deep breath.

"I . . . I love you, Ogino. Will you go out with me?"

I couldn't say it right. I couldn't look him in the eye, and hung my head. My voice sounded shaky. If I could somehow rewind time, I wished I could say it again. No, if I could, I would try to redo the whole night from the moment we saw each other. But that wasn't possible. You can't undo what you've already said.

I wondered if he'd truly heard me. I looked up nervously, and saw Ogino looking my way, with a stunned expression on his face. With his hand pressed to his forehead, he mumbled, "Um, I, uh . . ."

"Is that a no?"

"Um, Shizuku, are you serious?"

"Yes." I tried to keep my lips from trembling as I stared at him with all my might. Finally, the look of confusion disappeared from his face.

"I'm sorry, Shizuku," he said, looking right at me. "I just don't think of you that way. And I don't think I'll ever be able to. I'm not sure if I told you before, but I'm going out with someone."

After taking some time to digest what Ogino had said, I nodded. "I understand. Thank you for being up front about it."

"I'm sorry," Ogino repeated. He sounded genuinely apologetic, and hearing him made me want to apologize even more for putting him in that situation.

"No, I knew you'd turn me down. I'm sorry for springing it on you," I said, doing my best to smile.

"Really, that's not necessary . . . I'm sorry I had no idea. If I did something to give you the wrong impression, it's my fault. I'm sorry."

"You did nothing wrong, Ogino. Absolutely nothing."

Ogino was such a kind person. He was so kind I felt like I might cry. I was grateful it was nighttime. I could get by without him seeing my face.

"Heh heh heh, well, it's late," I said cheerfully, trying to dispel the heavy feeling in the air. "Shall we get going?"

"Yeah, okay . . ."

I felt sad, but it was also somehow refreshing. I felt at peace. It was like a wind had blown through and cleared away the thing that had been occupying my thoughts for days. "Hey, come on," I urged Ogino, who seemed not quite ready to go.

The two of us walked along the narrow path through the cemetery in silence. No one passed us now. We stayed like that, just the two of us, not saying a word, until we made it to the road. Ogino offered to walk me home, but I said, "I'm okay. It's not far."

"Well, okay, then. I'll see you later," Ogino said apologetically, as he stood there.

"Ogino, you're a very earnest person, and very sweet," I said, giggling.

"Huh, no, I . . ."

"You don't need to take my teenage girl nonsense too seriously. All the girls in school are into going out with older guys. I just got swept up in it."

"Is that right?" Ogino laughed weakly, still clearly troubled by it all.

"It was just a joke. I'd hate it if you got upset over this. So please don't let things get awkward and stop coming to the Torunka. If you do, my father will get mad at me."

Ogino scratched the back of his head in confusion. "You really gave me a shock. You shouldn't say something like that without thinking of the consequences. You should only say it to someone you truly love. You're like a little sister to me, so it really got me worried."

"I'm sorry."

Ogino was trying to give me advice as an adult, but I was pretending to take it lightly.

"Well, I'll be going, then. I'll see you later, Shizuku."

When he started to walk away, I reflexively called out to him, just as I had when we were saying goodbye the first day we ran into each other again. "Um..."

Ogino turned back a little beyond the streetlight. "What is it?"

"Are you happy these days?"

"Huh?" His eyes widened in surprise. "Um yeah, I think so," he said. "I hadn't really considered it, but I'm in good health, my job is going well, and I have someone in my life I really care about. So, in that sense, my life is fulfilling, and I think that's what happiness is."

As he looked at me, he had an expression on his face like someone who's been pranked by a child and doesn't know what to do about it.

"But what made you ask that all of a sudden?"

I smiled, satisfied with his answer. Then I said in a loud voice, "No reason. Okay, goodbye!" I waved goodbye and ran down the hill.

Ah, I felt so much lighter. I walked along, stretching my arms into the air, looking up at the stars twinkling in the night sky. It

A Drop of Love

was quiet, aside from the occasional car passing by. All the shops along the street—the rice cracker seller, the grocery store, the tsukudani shop—had their shutters down.

Deneb, Altair, Vega.

I searched the night sky for those familiar stars. Ever since I confessed my feelings for Ogino, it was like a breath of fresh air. My mind felt free and clear, and I was able to look back calmly on what I'd done. I guess you could say I was feeling like myself again.

What time was it? Was it too late to go by Kōta's house? As I walked along thinking it over, I heard a low male voice call out from the pitch-black road, "Hey!"

I let out a little scream.

A figure leaning against the guardrail up ahead said, "What the hell are you doing?"

"Wait, Kōta?"

Kōta was walking straight at me with a surly look on his face.

"What're you doing wandering the streets this time of night? Your dad is super worried about you!"

"Ah!" When I checked my phone, which I'd left in my pocket all this time, it had a crazy number of missed calls. That reminded me that I'd gone out without saying anything to my father. According to the time on my phone it was already close to ten o'clock. This was not good. He was definitely going to be mad at me. I started to rush.

"He called me too, and I told him we were so focused on the game we were playing that you hadn't noticed your phone. You can thank me now," Kōta said brusquely.

"Oh, th-thanks..."

He must've been trying to find me. Even though we hadn't

made up yet. Kōta was still giving me that surly look. But for some reason, just looking at him made me feel better.

"Hey, you'd better get home fast."

I rushed after Kōta, who was already trotting ahead.

"Were you with Ogino?" he asked without turning around.

"Yeah," I answered honestly.

"And what'd you tell him?"

"'I love you,' I said. 'Please be my boyfriend.' And it was a spectacular disaster." I giggled.

"Wow, you really drove right down the middle on that one," he said from up ahead, sounding surprised. "Well, there're better ways to go about these things, you know. You gotta hit 'em with a few body blows to soften them up."

"But this wasn't the kind of love that could last."

"Oh?"

"You were right to be worried about me. I think I was acting a little weird. When it gets to this time of year, it's hard to explain, but I get this urge to hold on to someone for dear life. If I don't, the grief will crush me . . ."

Kōta was walking ahead of me, so his back was facing me, but he quickly responded. "Hmmm . . . I see."

I spoke slowly as I tried to gather my thoughts. "This time I guess it was Ogino. Ogino loved my sister. So I figured why not me? I ended up acting kind of crazy, dressing in my sister's clothes. Yet it all seemed fine to me at the time. I thought if I could just take my sister's place . . . But, as things went on, my thinking got all screwed up . . ." I went on, explaining what happened not just to Kōta, but to myself as well, going over every word of the story for both of us. "I wasn't just in love with Ogino.

I was in love with what was left of my sister within him. Really, if Ogino had never been my sister's boyfriend, I don't think I would have fallen for him. When you said I was too fixated on my sister, that's what you meant, isn't it?"

Kōta didn't answer. He just kept on walking briskly down the hill. It didn't bother me, I was used to talking to his back by now.

"Which is why the way I fell in love was like coming down with the flu. Your fever spikes all of a sudden, but it only lasts a short while. And now, check it out—I don't look sad at all, do I?" I'd been going on and on, caught up in my monologue, when Kōta suddenly stopped short. It caught me off guard, and I immediately rammed into his back and fell forward.

"Ow! Why'd you stop all of a sudden?" I grumbled as I staggered around.

Kōta turned and scowled at me. "Are you an idiot?"

He had flung the words in my face the way he always did and now he was staring at me.

"Huh?"

"How long have we known each other? We've been together since we were babies. So you can try to laugh it off as much as you want, but all I see is how incredibly sad you are."

"Ah . . ." That's all it took for me to fall apart. "Ugh . . ." The sound came from my mouth, and the tears I'd been holding back all this time came flooding out. Big tears fell from my eyes, spilling from them like water, and I couldn't stop them.

I was crying, and the sounds I made were so loud it surprised even me. Standing in the deserted street, I lost all sense of shame and looked up at the sky and sobbed.

"It's true I never would've fallen for Ogino if he hadn't been my sister's boyfriend... But what I felt the past two weeks when I believed I was in love with him—that was real. Even if that's all it was, it was real," I said, thinking to myself, I must look terrible sobbing like this. I'm sure my face is a mess.

It was the first time in my life that I felt like I was in love. When I thought about Ogino, I was happy—I'm sure of that. But it was all over now. And those precious feelings that had built up inside me now had nowhere to go. There was no one to share them with. It seemed such an unbelievable shame, and it made me unbearably sad.

"That makes sense," Kōta murmured as he patted me on the shoulder. And that made me cry even more.

I looked up at the sky and sobbed so much it was like I was howling. I thought of how pitiful I was in love, and I cried with all my heart. I was like a child. And then I thought of how sad it was to be crying like this, and I cried more. Kōta didn't say anything else. He just stood at my side.

How long did we stay like that? When I finally stopped crying, I felt like all of the water had been wrung from my body. With no handkerchief in my pocket, my snot and tears ended up soaking my T-shirt and dripping onto the street beneath my feet.

I looked up and took a deep breath. "I'm sorry, Kōta," I said, my chest still heaving.

How can crying make you feel so lightheaded?

"Huh? It's okay. Nobody's looking anyway." Kōta was smirking at me, but his voice was kind.

"That's not what I meant. I mean, I'm sorry for what happened before. I said some terrible things. I've been wanting to apologize all this time."

A Drop of Love

Kōta hemmed and hawed. "You're not the only one to blame. I was being childish, not that I'm an adult or anything."

"I was really afraid that we'd never make up," I muttered, looking at my feet.

Beneath the streetlights we cast long shadows onto the asphalt. The shape of a hand reached out from Kōta's shadow and passed over the shadow of my head. At the same moment, I felt the warmth and then the weight of his hand on my head.

"Are you stupid? How could that even be possible? You really are losing it," Kōta said, talking big again.

"Stupid people shouldn't tell people they're stupid."

"Damn, you were being such a nice girl a second ago."

In the end, the two of us burst out laughing. Then as we went on insulting each other in our usual way, we started walking again, side by side. And the fight we'd been having up until a moment ago vanished without a trace.

The market street was right in front of us. But if I came home with my face looking like I'd just cried my eyes out, I'd only worry my father. "We could tell him the ending of the zombie game was incredibly moving," Kōta suggested.

"That'll never work." I laughed.

A car drove quietly by, gliding alongside us.

Though I'd told him I was fine, Kōta ended up walking me back to Torunka Street. "Thanks," I said

"It's on my way home," he said, looking the other way like he was embarrassed.

"That's not what I meant. I meant thanks for everything. I'm lucky you were there for me."

It was probably the first time in my life I'd ever formally thanked Kōta. Having gone through such a bewildering range of different emotions in the past few hours, I felt like the evil spirit that had taken over my body had vanished, and now I was myself again. The things I normally would have had a hard time saying to Kōta now came out easily.

"It might be a little late for that, but, hey, I promised Sumiré." Kōta was leaning against the closed shutter of the grocery store when he made this odd revelation.

"Huh, what're you talking about?" I said, raising my voice.

"Sumiré asked me to. When I went to see her at the hospital, she said, 'Look after Shizuku for me,'" Kōta said nonchalantly.

"What do you mean? I had no idea."

"Yeah, that's true. It was our secret," he said, even more nonchalantly. "Sumiré said, 'I might have turned out a little warped, but Shizuku's different. She's honest, and she has a beautiful heart. People are naturally drawn to her. She's had that rare talent ever since she was born. But she's so kind that she ends up getting hurt a lot. When that happens, look out for her, will you?'"

What was with this day? This was just too much for twenty-four hours.

"What did you say then?"

"I mean, what's the right thing to say to someone who's about to die? I told her, 'No problemo.'" He laughed. "I mean, I am a guy after all," he added, doing his best bodybuilder pose.

It was so ridiculous that I burst out laughing again.

"Ahhh, did I say that out loud? They're definitely going to kill me in heaven. Really though, I agree with Sumiré. I like that about you. So I hate seeing you trying to change who you are. You should be yourself. Do you know what I mean?"

"I do." I gave him a big nod.

"Okay, time for me to take a dump and go to bed."

Kōta walked away, leaving me with more information than I wanted to know.

After that, we went through some pretty hectic days as we prepared for the ceremony marking the sixth anniversary of my sister's death. My mother had come back temporarily for the event. Seeing her for the first time in eight months, after her last visit at New Year's, I thought she looked tan and healthy. The light was back in her eyes.

At the ceremony, we had to deal with a lot—we'd ordered a bento for each guest, but we were short one; our relatives said some unpleasant things to us, and it felt ten times more tiring than working at the café. But I managed not to get too run-down. Afterward, the three of us sat down to dinner for the first time in a long while, and talked about all kinds of things, and the next day, I saw my mother off at the airport.

In the afternoon, the train coming back from Narita to Nippori was empty. There were only a few scattered passengers on the train, so I got a seat near the middle, and sat watching the white clouds outside.

Sumiré

As I looked up at the blue sky, I spoke silently to my sister.

How is it over there?

I'm fine here.

When I said goodbye to Mom, she told me that she'd come back to live with us again next year. I said she could take her time. After all, just because we're apart doesn't mean we stop being a family. Don't you think?

Oh, and I meant to tell you that when I saw Ogino again, I finally understood what you were up to. I couldn't decide whether I should tell Ogino the whole story, but in the end, I didn't say anything. The truth is you never actually disliked Ogino, did you?

I saw what really happened. I saw you in your room in the hospital, holding the book he'd given you to your chest and crying. It seemed strange then, but now I understand. You broke up with him because you knew you didn't have much time left. You wanted to avoid putting him through the experience of watching you die. That's so like you. But you should know that Ogino told me he's happy now. He was smiling. Isn't that great? That's what you really wanted, isn't it?

I'm being myself too. They say it's hard to work on yourself, but I'm taking my time. So I can live up to the promise of my name. I tried my best, but I realize now that I can't be like you. So, I'm fine being who I am. Keep an eye out for me, will you?

The train sped on, racing me back home to my neighborhood.

When I get back to the Torunka, I'm going to have a cup of coffee.

I'm not sure why I suddenly got the urge, but I wanted my father to make me a hot cup of coffee. Fill the white cup to the brim. I wonder how he'll react when I ask him to make me a cup.

Outside the window, the landscape flew by. As hard as it was to believe after the last several days, my mind was now calm and clear.

But I won't forget that I was in love, however briefly it lasted. Deeply in love. And it's something I'll treasure. Even if the pain returns, it won't be so bad. Someday, I know, I'll fall in love again.

And until that day, I'll be building up my confidence. So that when the time comes, whoever it is will see me for who I am.

Just as I was thinking this, Kōta's stupid face popped into my head. I immediately dismissed the thought. No way. Never going to happen. Not Kōta. Impossible. Besides, it seemed clear that it would be a while before I fell in love again.

But now, it was time for some coffee. As soon as I got home, that's the first thing I needed to do. And if it gave me nightmares, I'd just chase them away. My life until this moment had made me tough. I could handle it.

What would my first coffee in ten years taste like?

I stared out the window, feeling just a tiny bit nervous.

Translator's Note

Ayako tends to have her own idiosyncratic version of her favorite quotations, but I've tracked down the originals for readers who might want to seek them out. The first time we meet Ayako, she quotes Matthew 7:7, "Knock and the door shall be opened unto you," and Jean-Jacques Rousseau's *Émile*: "To live is not merely to breathe but to take action." ("*Vivre, ce n'est pas respirer, c'est agir.*").

"Life is a get-together to which one is never invited twice" is from the German writer Hans Carossa. The full version of the original quotation, which appears in *Führung und Geleit*, is "*Leben ist eine Zusammenkunft, zu der immer nur eine begrenzte Zahl auf einmal geladen ist, und nie wird die Einladung wiederholt.*"

"Do not, for one repulse, forgo the purpose that you have resolved t'effect" is said by Antonio in Shakespeare's *The Tempest*. Readers familiar with the play will remember that what Sebastian is being urged to do is far less wholesome than Ayako's plan to turn Hiro's life around.

"The world is a fine place and worth the fighting for" is something Robert Jordan says to himself near the end of Ernest Hemingway's *For Whom the Bell Tolls*.

"O, 'tis Love that makes us blissful. O, 'tis Love that makes us rich" ("*O, die Liebe macht uns selig/ O, die Liebe macht uns reich!*")

is from Heinrich Heine's "Zum Polterabend." (My thanks to Rey Akdogan and Craig Buckley for helping me fine-tune these German-to-Japanese-to-English translations.)

"Write it on your heart that every day is the best day in the year" is from Ralph Waldo Emerson's essay, "Works and Days."

Not long ago, I went searching for the Torunka Café, the *kissaten* at the heart of Satoshi Yagisawa's latest book. In the story, the café is located at the end of a narrow backstreet in downtown Tokyo in a site so hidden away that few travelers ever find it. At least two characters in the book mention that they first stumbled across it by following a stray cat down the alley. I wandered through the narrow, winding streets of Yanaka, past markets, bakeries, and food stands, but no cat offered to show me the way.

In the book, the café is quite small, with some seats at the counter and a handful of tables, but like the Morisaki Bookshop, it's the center of a community of people for whom it becomes a second home.

Time seems to move differently at the Torunka Café. There's time to savor a cup of coffee, to reminisce, to confess a secret, or to read a book like this one, which celebrates the pleasures of the *junkissa*, a term that encompasses both those cafés with the quaint charm of the Shōwa period as well as those devoted to the perfect cup of coffee. In the book, the Torunka Café combines the best of both. It still has the classic pink rotary pay phone and a pendulum clock on the wall, but the coffee is made by the owner with such careful attention that it gives one character in the book a sign that there's something in this world worth fighting for. The speakers play Chopin's piano études. The regulars

Translator's Note

stop by for a cup of coffee at their usual times. It's here that we meet the book's characters.

When I met with the book's author, Satoshi Yagisawa, after my search, I asked him about the café's hidden location. I'm sworn to secrecy and cannot reveal any more here, for places like that are best discovered on one's own. We seem to find them right when we need them.

I am grateful to the people I found right when I needed them: Sara Nelson and Edie Astley at HarperCollins; Zoe Yang at Bonnier Books; Andrea Blatt and Dara Kaye at WME; my friends Junko Suzuki and Ayaka Kamei, who offered invaluable insights; Melissa Ozawa and Bruno Navasky, who carefully combed through the manuscript; and my wife, Nicole, who is always my first reader.

Eric Ozawa

READ MORE BY
SATOSHI YAGISAWA

"Readers will pick this up for the atmosphere of this well-established world. They will turn the last page with a deepened love for this bookshop family and how well they care for each other and their customers and neighbors."
— *Booklist*

"A familiar romance about books and bookstores, told with heart and humor."
—*Kirkus Reviews*

HARPER PERENNIAL

DISCOVER GREAT AUTHORS, EXCLUSIVE OFFERS, AND MORE AT HC.COM.